"Fast-paced, action-packed, and full of mysteries, *Death, Doom, and Detention* is a solid sequel that should keep fans of the series turning the pages long into the night."
—*YA Books Central*

"Jones's Darklight series features all of the same attitude and humor as her adult series, but with a cast of teen characters, making it fun for adult fans as well as teens." —*BookBitch*

"Darynda Jones manages to write a completely unique story about a girl who's lost in her own way, an angel who's darker than he seems, and a prophecy that's scaring everyone and anyone. It seems like your typical story, but it's far from it!"
—*Fiction Freak*

"The plot, setting, and theme are all tied together nicely to make this book a fast-paced, enjoyable novel. You'll smile, you'll groan, you'll laugh, you might even want to throw the book down in anger. Basically, you will fall even more in love with this series." —*Miss Literati*

"This sequel starts out with a bang and never stops."
—*Night Owl Reviews*

"Action-packed, intriguing, and exciting . . . I cannot wait to see what Ms. Jones has in store for us in book three, *Death and the Girl He Loves*." —*Fresh Fiction*

"Darynda continues her winning streak with *Death, Doom, and Detention*. . . . Jones's writing—in any genre—is a breath of fresh air." —*Suspense Magazine*

Praise for *Death and the Girl Next Door*

"Unique, witty, and touching—I LOVED THIS BOOK!"
—P. C. Cast, *New York Times* bestselling
author of the House of Night series

"Outrageously funny, sinfully sexy, with a cast of characters that steals your heart from the very first page . . . I loved this book!" —Inara Scott, author of the
Delcroix Academy series

"*Death and the Girl Next Door* is unputdownable. Darynda Jones breathes fresh life into the young adult genre with exciting twists to legends we only think we understand and edgy, compelling characters you can't help but care about."
—Gwen Hayes, author of *Falling Under*

"Only Darynda Jones could make the Angel of Death crush-worthy! Wickedly sharp with brilliant wit, *Death and the Girl Next Door* will leave you craving more!"
—Lara Chapman, author of *Flawless*

"Snapping with sarcasm and a pitch-perfect voice, Darynda Jones has brought her signature humor and supernatural sass to Riley High. Trust me, there's nothing grim about this reaper!" —Roxanne St. Claire, *New York Times*
bestselling author of *Don't You Wish*

"*Death and the Girl Next Door* delivers a smokin' hot story and a guy to die for. Darynda Jones gives one candy-smacking, awesome read that won't let you go until the end."
—Shea Berkley, author of *The Marked Son*

ALSO BY DARYNDA JONES

Fifth Grave Past the Light
Death, Doom, and Detention
Death and the Girl Next Door
Fourth Grave Beneath My Feet
Third Grave Dead Ahead
Second Grave on the Left
First Grave on the Right

death and the girl he loves

DARYNDA JONES

 ST. MARTIN'S GRIFFIN ⚞ NEW YORK

This is a work of fiction. All of the characters, organizations,
and events portrayed in this novel are either products of the author's
imagination or are used fictitiously.

www.stmartins.com

Design by Anna Gorovoy

The Library of Congress Cataloging-in-Publication Data
is available upon request.

ISBN 978-0-312-62522-1 (trade paperback)
ISBN 978-1-250-03843-2 (e-book)

First Edition: October 2013

10 9 8 7 6 5 4 3 2 1

In loving memory of "Ms. Mullins"
(aka Mary Lydia Mullins-Lynch)

Everyone is born with an internal lamp,
a spark that is wild and feral and luminous.
Some people hide it, bury it deep inside their souls,
smother it until over time it dulls and crumbles to dust.

Others share it.
They've learned that by using it to nurture and to nourish,
it shines all the brighter. Burns all the hotter.

Then you have those who set it free.
They sacrifice a part of themselves and watch in
delirious glee as their spark ignites fires in
hundreds of others.

Those people are called teachers.
Thank you for being one of mine.

ACKNOWLEDGMENTS

Here's the thing. I have this sister. She's a bit quirky but has this effervescence about her. This awesomeness. Then I have these brothers. Same story. Different package. Quirky. Awesome. The whole bit. And there's a husband in there, too, who makes me feel like I almost deserve all the incredible things that happen to me despite everything. Throw in two beautiful sons, a few cousins and in-laws and other extended family members, toss in a whole slew of friends, chapter mates, sisters-in-arms, publicity and marketing peeps, producers, artists, copy editors, an assistant who runs circles around me, a street team that makes me believe in magic, an agent who I'm pretty sure the word "magnificent" was coined for, and an editor whose work ethics put world leaders to shame, and I am sitting smack dab in the middle of this cauldron of nourishment, creativity, and positive energy. That right there is what we call a support system, and I have the best in the world, hands down.

And then there's you. The reader. The incandescent being who thrives on words like others thrive on caffeinated beverages. Because of you, I get to make up stories for a living.

Thank you so much, everyone.

You know who you are.

You know what you mean to me.

You know I'd be locked in a padded cell without you.

We should do lunch!

death and the girl he loves

SAME DAY, DIFFERENT DEATH

The Bedford Fields Academy pitched itself as one of the most prestigious private schools in North America, promising a stellar education and a future brighter than an exploding supernova. Or something along those lines. In reality, it was a last-ditch effort for rich parents with kids who'd been kicked out of every other institution in the free world. The boarding school was insanely expensive, but those parents with unruly children and money to burn would pay anything for the illusion of a good education. They took their public guise seriously.

Keeping up the pretense of good parentage took effort. And trust funds. And the school kept the children out of their hair. For that, they would pay extra.

I didn't know that when I started at Bedford Fields, of course, but a pretty blonde with too much eyeliner and too few scruples explained the rules and regulations of the school in the bathroom while cleaning her nails with a switchblade. She'd lifted the knife from a vendor while on vacation with her family in Cabo San Lucas the summer before, and she made sure to mention how she'd honed the blade to a razor's edge for ease of penetration. She then proceeded to ask me why a redheaded short chick with pasty white skin dared to enter her domain. I had no idea if she meant the school or the bathroom. Either way, that was my first day and my introduction to life sans everything I'd ever known. It went downhill from there.

First of all, the reality of winter in the North was a complete shock to my system. I couldn't get warm, even bundled in seven layers as I was then. Second, I'd started school in the middle of the semester, thus I was behind in almost every class they'd assigned to me. And third, I apparently had an accent, a fact that some of the more irritating students reveled in teasing me about.

But the worst part of all was that I took homesickness to a whole new level. I missed my grandparents, my friends, my house, and my old school to the point of feeling like I had the flu 24/7. I even missed Tabitha Sind, the bane of my existence. Luckily I had Kenya here to take up where Tab had left off. At least Tabitha had never threatened me with a switchblade. Life was simpler in New Mexico. Life at a boarding school for rich kids in a state where the weather rivaled that of Siberia was far too complex. And hazardous to my health.

"Lorraine!"

I heard my nom de guerre but kept walking. While my friends in New Mexico knew me as Lorelei McAlister, aka my real name, the students and faculty here in Maine knew me as Lorraine Pratt, a transfer student from Arizona. Fortunately, I'd been to Arizona a couple of times, just enough to fend off questions from the more curious students.

"Lorraine," she called again, but I hated nothing more than being late to class. These teachers at BFA could wither a winter rose with one look.

I kept my head down and my gaze glued to the floor. Now that I was no longer a novelty, I could slip relatively unnoticed from class to class. At first, everyone stared. Everyone. That's what I got for transferring in the middle of a semester. But once the other kids found out I was a scholarship student, and not a particularly interesting one at that, they stopped staring and ignored me altogether. Most of them, anyway.

I could handle being ignored, but the scholarship was a mystery I had yet to figure out. I'd been secreted away from everything I'd ever known in the middle of the night. Driven in four different vehicles with four different groups of caretakers for over two days straight, and delivered onto the steps of Bedford Fields in the bitingly frigid predawn hours with little more than a suitcase and a hair tie. How on earth did I suddenly have a scholarship? That was clearly a part of the plan my grandparents forgot to mention.

"Lorraine, wait up."

I finally slowed, risking death by trampling in the crowded hall, and let the eighth-grader, who also happened to be my roommate, catch up to me. She was the only student still enamored with my shiny newness, and she was the only kid besides a boy named Wade who paid me any mind. I'd been at the boarding school for weeks, and Wade treated me like we'd known each other forever, but Crystal still looked at me with stars in her eyes. Hopefully my gleam would wear off soon, because she could be a little irritating.

She beamed at me when she caught up, her cerulean eyes sparkling behind round-rimmed glasses and thick dark braids.

Well, irritating in a charming way. She was another scholarship student, a science whiz who was destined to be the next Stephen Hawking if I had anything to say about it. The girl's mind was like a supercomputer on steroids.

"Hey, Crystal."

"Hey," she said back, breathless from trying to catch up to me. "So what are you doing?"

I tried not to chuckle and indicated the door ahead of me with an index finger. "Just headed to class."

"Oh, right, okay, that's a good idea. Last class of the day."

"Yup. And isn't yours across campus?" I asked her.

She looked around in utter cluelessness, spun in a complete circle to get her bearings. I felt the crush of students acutely, especially when one student knocked me forward as he rushed past. I felt a tug at my coat and started to say something, but I barely caught sight of the back of his head before he disappeared into the crowd. He was wearing a hoodie anyway.

"Yes, it is." Crystal's pale face had a light sprinkling of freckles over cheeks slightly chapped from the biting winds of Maine. Under a button nose sat a bow-shaped mouth that made her look even younger than her fourteen years. She looked like a doll I once had. *Exactly* like a doll I once had. It was eerie. She put one foot behind the other and hitched a thumb over her shoulder. "I guess I should jet, then."

I couldn't help a grin. "Okay, you jet. I'll see you later?"

After flashing me a smile that could have melted the heart of the White Witch in Narnia, she nodded and hurried away.

I watched her leave, a little enamored myself with such a guileless creature, then turned and ran right into the one girl in school I did *not* want to run into. The only one who accessorized with black nail polish, a razor-blade pendant, and a switchblade.

She gaped, completely offended by my presence, then shoved me away from her. I stumbled back and barely kept from tumbling head over heels by grabbing on to another student's backpack. He scowled over his shoulder, then jerked out of my grip before I could apologize. Or right myself. I almost fell anyway, but I managed to get my footing without any more humiliation than absolutely necessary.

"Nice save," Kenya said, raising her brows as though impressed.

But I was still reeling from what I'd gained from our little encounter. I wasn't fond of Kenya Slater. She wasn't fond of me. But it was disturbing nonetheless to watch her die.

Unfortunately for me—and everyone around me—I have, for lack of a better word, *visions.* Sometimes when I touch people, I can see into their futures or their pasts. It's heart-wrenching on several levels. I never see the time they were laughing at a party or riding a roller coaster at the fair, screaming with exhilaration. No, I see the bad parts of their lives. I see the catastrophic. I see the pain and fear and anxiety. And now, thanks to this nifty skill I'd inherited, I knew exactly when, where, and how Kenya was going to die.

Her death flashed before my eyes the moment we touched. The visions were thoughtful that way. And now I had a decision to make. I'd struggled with the question of divulgence before. Many times. And this scenario was no exception. I might be able to prevent her death if she'd listen to me, but that took a lot of faith. And since she threatened me with a switchblade every chance she got, I didn't figure faith was her strong suit. Especially faith in me. The new girl. The girl she most liked to harass and promise a slow and painful death to. I was pretty sure I'd developed a nervous twitch after meeting her.

But this was different. Maybe it was a timing thing. She was going to die too soon. Too young. She literally had only days to live. And the vision stole my breath with its vividness.

In it, a storm rolled in, darkening what had been a sunny afternoon. She was on a boat with her aunt, uncle, big sister, and little brother, but it wasn't a vacation or a pleasure trip. She was scared. Her aunt and uncle were scared, too—terrified, in fact—running, trying to get away from something, to escape. The clouds roiling overhead like a cauldron of a dark witch's brew dipped lower and lower in the sky. If Kenya reached up, she could have touched them, but she was busy clinging to her brother for dear life. The water churned and crashed against her uncle's sailboat. Rain slashed horizontally through the sky, the stinging chill cutting to the bone. Her sister had wedged herself between two seats, huddled there, shivering, worried she'd fall overboard.

I could feel the unimaginable fear that blinded Kenya to everything but those clouds. Yet it wasn't the storm clouds she was afraid of. It was something else. Something inside them.

Before I could identify the source of her fear, another wave hit. It slammed against the boat, causing one side to tip and rise with the swell until the small boat had no choice but to succumb to the fates. The water hit Kenya hard, slapping against her as she crashed into it. She tried desperately to keep ahold of her brother, reached blindly for her sister, but the pull of the waves was too strong. It sucked her deeper and deeper into its icy grip. She kicked. Fought with every ounce of strength she had. Then, left with no choice, she exchanged water for air and filled her burning lungs. Panic seized her with such a violent force, she gagged, tried to swallow the entire ocean, searched desperately for oxygen in the thick liquid. And found none.

The last image that flashed in my mind was of her floating in the deep gray depths of the arctic water. Her eyes open. Her mouth a grim line as though she'd accepted her fate at last, but did so unhappily.

And she knew. She knew who was to blame.

Ricocheting back to the present, I sucked in a sharp gulp of air, fighting the feeling of suffocation, of drowning. I doubled over and coughed, then clamped a hand over my mouth when I felt bile slip up the back of my throat.

What were they running from? Why were they so scared? And why would anyone be the blame for a storm?

"Pratt?" she said, her voice edged with wariness instead of her usual menace.

I ignored her, turned, and was fighting my way to the bathroom when I bumped into a boy. Another vision gripped me and performed a hostile takeover of all brain function. And just like the vision of Kenya and her family, this boy's expiration date was rocketing toward him. And it was disturbingly similar to hers. The storm. The dark clouds. The roaring winds. The boy was running toward his dorm on the school campus, but unlike Kenya, he was scared of the storm and nothing else. He died when a tree was uprooted and took down some electrical wires near him. The currents hammering through his body brought me down, because I didn't just see what happened to people in my visions; I felt it, too. Every spike of fear. Every wince of anguish. Every spasm of pain. And being electrocuted to death hurt. An agonizing pain pulsated through me, attacking my nervous system until the boy breathed his last breath and his body shut down.

I felt a hand on my arm. I pushed it away and stumbled to my feet, reeling from that experience when another boy reached to help me.

Same day.

Same storm.

Same utter chaos.

Different death.

I jerked away from him and slammed into a girl. I now had an audience. Students surrounded me, and every one I touched died.

Same day.

Same storm.

Same utter chaos.

Different death.

One after the other until I stumbled into a bathroom and locked myself in a stall. The shock of each death shuddered through me as I heaved my lunch into the toilet. When the spasms eased, I spit out the sour taste and tried to clear my head. To understand what I was seeing.

Something had changed. Something had happened in the last few minutes that altered the fates of every kid at school. But they were in different places. On the water. In a storm shelter. In Town Hall. Fleeing the country in a chartered Learjet. And it wasn't just them. It was their brothers and sisters, their parents and friends. In exactly five days, everyone in the city of Bangor, Maine, was going to die. But somehow, I didn't think it would stop there.

What was different? What could have—?

Then it hit me. The boy. The tug at my coat. I reached into my pocket and pulled out a note. It was the third one I'd received in quite the same manner. Stuffed into the pocket of my jacket when I wasn't looking or secreted into my backpack.

Dread consumed me as I opened it. This one had a stick figure drawing of two people, a boy and a girl. The girl—who I was going to assume was me since she had garishly curly red hair—was lying on the ground, presumably dead. Blood pooled on her chest and sat in puddles around her head and torso. The boy clutched a knife in his three-fingered hand, but he was leaning over her. Over me. And a darkness was leaving her mouth and entering his. Like he wanted what was inside me. Like he welcomed it.

And somehow he knew. When I was six years old, I had been possessed by a demon. A demon that was still inside me. But no one here knew that. How could they? And yet this boy did.

Five words made up the text of the note. I read them over and over in disbelief. Fear darkened the edges of my periphery. Five words. Five words that had the power to make the darkness inside me quake and buck inside my body. Five words that would change the fate of the world. Five words that read simply, *I know what you are.*

THROUGH THE GATES
OF HELL DARKLY

I know what you are. Not "who." What.

Admittedly, the "what" part was way more interesting than the "who." And I'd found out myself only a couple of months prior. Though I'd had visions my whole life—premonitions, one could say—I only recently found out I was apparently a prophet. I was the last prophet, in fact, that hailed from a long line of female prophets that dated back hundreds of years, beginning with my ancestor Arabeth, the first woman in human history to be burned at the stake as a witch.

Historically, anytime a woman had the gift of premonition, she was a witch. Anytime a man was born with the gift, he was a prophet. Least that was the way I saw it, and the injustice did not escape me. I'd thought of it often while holed up in a boarding school a thousand miles from my home with nothing better to do than to consider the injustice of pretty much everything on earth. World hunger. War. School uniforms. But before I left my hometown of Riley's Switch, New Mexico, a group of descendants of true nephilim—beings that were part human, part angel—killed people while trying to get to me. People I'd known since I was a kid. People I'd loved. My leaving was for the best. I couldn't let anyone else get hurt because of me. My chest constricted painfully every time I thought about it, and yet it constricted more when I thought about how I missed my home.

Putting all that aside, how could anyone at Bedford Fields know who I was? What I was? What I had inside me? I figured I could hang in the bathroom for the next two days and try to figure it out, but loitering was frowned upon in this institution.

Knowing I'd be chastised in front of the whole class for being late, I decided to go to the nurse's office instead, if for no other reason than to buy myself some time to think. My legs wobbled as I staggered to the sink and rinsed out my mouth. Then the door opened and someone walked straight up to me. I recognized the long legs of Kenya instantly and half expected a switchblade to be glimmering in her hand. Instead, she dropped my backpack at my feet. With the threat of imminent death gone, I splashed water on my face and reached for a paper towel.

"What's wrong?" Kenya asked, and again the usual menace was absent from her voice. Her tone wasn't exactly caring, but it wasn't threatening either.

"Nothing," I said before reaching for my backpack.

She put a foot on it, held it to the ground, so I straightened, too exhausted to negotiate the terms of my surrender.

"What?" I asked, weariness evident in my voice. The fight in me fled the premises every time I had a vision that strong, that blindingly real, but I normally had only one at a time. I'd never been bombarded to such a degree. One was enough to knock me on my butt. Several in a row were enough to put me in a coma; I was certain of it. Yet there I stood. Facing off against the mean girl, not worried in the least. What could she do to me that wouldn't happen in five days anyway? Or even sooner if Death Threat Guy had his way. Clearly, I'd jumped out of the frying pan and into the fire. I should've just stayed in Riley's Switch, where I at least had friends and family. I had no one here. Several weeks into my stay, I still had no one I could turn to in times like this. Then again, who would believe me?

I figured I could stand there feeling sorry for myself, burst into tears lamenting the depths of my aloneness, or I could get in a fight with the mean girl. It was probably time. I'd pretty much met my quota of death threats for the day. If I were going to get my ass kicked, I'd darned sure go down swinging.

Then another thought hit. Since when did I even *think* the word "ass"? This school was a bad influence.

Another girl walked in. Kenya glanced over her shoulder, then slowly, reluctantly, disengaged her foot. I picked up my backpack before she could change her mind and headed toward the nurse's office. Or, as it was called here, the infirmary.

I could feel Kenya's gaze burning into my back as I walked

out and down the hall. That girl needed to adjust her meds before she had an aneurysm. Then again, in five days, it wouldn't matter.

Since I had no fever and there were no signs of an infection or a virus, the nurse wasn't sure whether to believe I'd just emptied my stomach into a toilet or not. But when she touched me and her death rushed into me, clenching my gut, causing me to hurtle toward her wastebasket and dry-heave into it for a full minute, she shut up, put a cool cloth on my forehead, and darkened the room to let me get some rest. Outside, clouds hung low and blocked what little sun might have filtered into the room through a small window above the nurse's desk.

Normally, the low light would have been comforting, but the nurse's death was worse than the rest. Death was hard to see anyway—surreal, unwanted—but hers was darker, more brutal. The black figures from the storm entered her and systematically broke her bones. One by one, her own muscles spasmed, jerked, and contracted until her fragile bones snapped under the pressure. An agonizing jolt of pain shot through her with each break. Causing her body to spasm more. Her spine to bow. Her ribs to crack. Her lungs filled with her own bodily fluids and she could no longer scream. She lay in a contorted heap of limbs and torso until the sweet release of death came when she drowned in her own blood.

I swallowed the bile burning the back of my throat. Fought the feeling of drowning and drew in long gulps of air. The infirmary smelled like sanitary hand gel. It was a clean scent and helped calm my stomach.

So the clouds were not clouds at all. The darkness was a

plethora of spirits that had escaped onto this plane, just as they had when I was six. The gates of hell had been opened before, and I'd seen it in a premonition when I was barely old enough to pick out my own clothes. I'd led my parents there, hoping they could close the lightninglike fissure in the sky, the one through which beings as black as midnight were escaping from their plane and onto ours. A demon came through. One demon, and after my parents disappeared into the fissure, after they vanished, the demon dematerialized and I breathed him in. His essence scorched my throat and filled my lungs, and he'd been inside me ever since.

But even then, the spirits didn't enter people and torture them as they had in my visions. Maybe spirits were like people. Maybe some were worse than others. Meaner. Sociopathic. Or were they demons? The demon that entered me was a massive, shining black guardian of the underworld. I wondered if a demon had entered the nurse—her death was so horrific—or if it was a spirit. A fallen angel or a former human. The demon that entered me did nothing to harm me. Not ever, but I'd been told my experience was extremely unusual. Since I had nothing to compare it to, I couldn't have said one way or the other.

I lay there with my eyes closed, not sleeping but replaying the visions over and over in my mind. After seeing that, after hearing the snap of bones, feeling the rip of flesh as the jagged ends protruded out of the nurse's limbs and torso, I figured I would never sleep again.

I turned onto my side, peeked out from under the cloth, and unzipped a side pocket on my navy backpack. My fingers found what they sought instantly. A picture I'd copied from an old annual, one that had actually captured the Angel of Death scoping out his next assignment, which happened to

be at Riley High in 1977. Of course, no one but my friends
from back home and I knew that. He looked like any other
student, only with muscles that rose and dipped magnifi-
cently and eyes that glimmered with an intelligence far beyond his presumed years.

A crowd of students stood around the flagpole of the old
high school. They were laughing, as though in disbelief, at
what must have been some kind of a prank. Mr. Davis, the
principal at my old alma matter, Riley High, had an older
brother named Elliot. When Elliot was in high school, he
and some friends had chained themselves to the pole and
were holding a sign that I still couldn't quite make out.

But they were laughing, too. Every student in the photo
was laughing, except one. A boy. He was standing closer to
the camera yet apart from the rest, his stance guarded, his
expression void, and as always, my gaze gravitated toward the
image of Jared Kovach.

He looked exactly like he did now. Same boyishly handsome face. Same mussed hair. Same T-shirt with the sleeves
rolled up, his arms long and sculpted like a swimmer's. There
was no mistaking the wide shoulders, the solid build, the
dark glint in Jared's eyes. Even the bands of tattoos peeked
out from under his shirtsleeves, the rows of angelic script
that encircled each of his biceps. He was just as breathtaking
back then, just as surreal.

The first time my best friends and I saw that picture in a
yearbook from the '70s, we had a difficult time swallowing
the fact that it was the same guy. Until we learned what Jared
was. Why he was there in the first place. He'd been sent for
Elliot Davis much the same way he'd been sent for me. That
was his job, after all. That's what the Angel of Death did. He
answered prayers, keeping people safe when they might have

died or tweaking the timing, nudging it a bit, in an effort to keep someone else safe who died as a result of the first person's tragedy.

For me, his mission was to take me sooner than nature would demand. On the day Jared showed up in Riley's Switch, I was hit by a truck, flew fifty feet in the air, and landed on solid concrete, sliding several more feet before crashing into a lamppost. With bones crushed and organs pulverized, I lay there as Jared came to stand over me. He kneeled down, and instead of taking me, per his orders, he brought me back to life. I felt it flow into me from his touch, warm and revitalizing.

I found out later why he'd been sent. His presence was in answer to the prayers of a little girl who just wanted her father to come home safe. But because I would've still been alive when the ambulance arrived, because I would've been medevaced to Albuquerque in a futile attempt to save my life, because my grandparents, in their haste to see me, would've sped through the mountain pass, crossing the center line and having a head-on with the little girl's father, Jared was sent to take me sooner. The little girl's father would've died peripherally, as a direct result of my getting hit by that truck. Jared's mission was to take me before I ever made it to the hospital, before the helicopter was even called, but he'd disobeyed those orders and saved me instead. Much to my glee. As a result, however, because he broke one of the three celestial laws of his kind—he'd changed human history—Jared was now stuck on earth as punishment, helping a group of us fight an upcoming war. This war. The war I'd just seen in my visions.

Or at least that was the plan before I ran off into the night. I thought that perhaps by disappearing, I would change the future. The war wouldn't happen.

Clearly, I'd made a mistake.

The war was going to happen anyway. My running did nothing to deter it. I was hoping that all the prophecies were wrong. The ones that said the last prophet of Arabeth, aka me, was going to stop a supernatural war before it ever started. I didn't know how to stop a war, supernatural or otherwise, and if my visions were correct, that meant the prophecies were wrong. I was about to stop absolutely nothing.

With sadness weighing me down, I touched the picture, let my fingertips slide along the cool surface until it paused on Jared. Then I took a deep breath, concentrated on the image, and dived inside.

When I first began entering pictures, there was a kind of curtain, a barrier I had to get past. That was no longer the case. I could now enter any picture in a matter of seconds. I barely had to concentrate anymore, I'd become so proficient at it.

And this particular picture, I'd entered at least a hundred times. Maybe two. I knew what was waiting for me. I had memorized the roar of laughter and idle chitchat. I automatically squinted my eyes, trying to block out the blinding sun, even though I could only see in. I was not physically there. I couldn't really squint my eyes or raise my hand to block it.

Just like every other time, I entered the scene at the exact same moment. I felt the heat of the New Mexico sun rush over me. It was warm and comforting, so opposite the damp, cold air of Maine. And the fact that I could feel the sun at all was new. When I first began, I could only see into the picture. Could only hear voices, music, birds . . . whatever gems the picture held. But now I could feel things. The heat in the air. The texture of the brick building Jared was leaning against. The soft breeze as it ruffled his hair. And I could manipulate my vantage point. I could look around, see things that were not in the picture itself.

I looked up at the boys chained to the flagpole. The sign that I could never make out in the picture read STATE CHAMPIONSHIP OR BUST. I'd learned that it was actually part of a skit for a pep rally they were having outside. The football team was going to the championship playoffs, and the school was sending them off in style. Elliot Davis, the team's quarterback, died barely an hour after this picture was taken. I wondered what it did to the rest of the team. How his death affected the players. I knew that they didn't win state that year, but I wondered if they even went. If they played at all.

I glanced to the side and saw the now familiar faces of the cheerleaders as well as several other students, mostly girls, looking toward what they must have thought was a new kid at school. But Jared was not there to attend class. He had been sent for Elliot and was . . . what? Stalking his prey? Biding his time? Did he like to watch humans interact? Did we fascinate him? Repulse him? I couldn't help but wonder what he thought of us.

I moved forward until I was standing beside him. The thing about going into these pictures was that I was a ghost. No one could see me. No one could hear me. I was simply an observer. I could not interact or alter my surroundings or change the outcome. I could only watch.

And yet, Jared could see me.

"I thought you were going to stop doing this."

I turned to look at him.

"Why are you here?" I asked. I'd thought of the question only recently, but now it burned inside me. "Why did you show up to take Elliot Davis an hour before his time when you can appear, take a person, and disappear within the span of a heartbeat?"

He regarded me from underneath his long lashes, and said quietly, "I came to see you."

I blinked in surprise. "I don't understand. How could you—?"

"You look tired," he said, interrupting.

"I'm fine."

The barest hint of a smile lifted the corners of his mouth. He leaned over and whispered into my ear. "Go to sleep."

Before I could protest, the world fell away and oblivion, that dark vortex of nothingness, swallowed me whole. It was comforting and warm. I hadn't been warm in weeks, and I suddenly felt as though I weren't alone at all. As though I'd never been alone.

"Lorraine?"

My lids fluttered open and I peered into the darkness, waiting for my eyes to adjust. When they did, I saw a pale face with round-rimmed glasses and a light dusting of freckles. Crystal gazed down at me, her blue eyes huge with worry. I lay there a moment, trying to gain my bearings, then bolted upright, almost head-butting her in the process. The world was about to end and I was napping. Napping!

Crystal almost fell back, her arms flailing for something to grab on to. She regained her balance, then said hurriedly, "I'll get you some water. Would you like some water? I'll get you some water." She jumped up to grab a cup just as reality crashed through the surface.

"Someone's trying to kill me!" I said, staring straight ahead in astonishment. "And the world is going to end."

She paused, bit her bottom lip in thought, gestured toward the cup. "So, no water?"

I swung my legs over the side of the cot and she hustled forward to help me stand. After swaying a little, however, I sat back down, the effects of the visions still weighing heavily.

"Should I get the nurse?" she asked.

I closed my eyes. Inhaled. Fought to regain my balance. This had happened before. The worst was when I saw a classmate die of thirst in the desert. Death by dehydration was not a good way to go, and I was thankful when Crystal drew me a cup of water anyway.

She put it in my shaking hands before sitting beside me on the cot. "Did you say someone is trying to kill you?"

Apparently parched, I emptied the cup in three gulps, then handed it back to her. She rose to refill it, then took up position beside me again. I was short for my height and Crystal was actually a tad taller than me, yet I couldn't help but think of her as small, childlike. It was her innocence. Her inquisitive disposition. So when her brows cinched together, her expression grave, and she said, "You know you can tell me anything, right?" I was surprised at how mature she sounded. How concerned.

I nodded and decided to let her into my warped little world. Even though I probably shouldn't have, I took out the note and showed it to her. I simply didn't know what else to do. Who else to talk to.

"Do you recognize this artist?" I asked.

She studied it, turning her head this way and that, then said, "My nephew draws like this, but he's not usually so morbid. Is that supposed to be you?" She pointed to the stick figure on the ground covered in blood.

"That's my take on it, yes."

She turned her head again, furrowed her brows in concentration. I wanted to hug her, she was so adorable, but that would mean touching her. That would mean getting a vision. I didn't want to see her death. I didn't want to see the deaths of her friends or family members, the devastation and fear in her eyes, so I stayed insulated with several inches between us.

"What is he doing?" she asked, indicating the dark matter leaving my mouth and entering my attacker's. "Why is he throwing up on you?"

Surprised, I regarded the picture again and realized that is exactly how it would look to someone who didn't know what was inside me. Who didn't know how it entered my body or the fact that it would probably exit the same way.

"I have no idea," I said.

"That's just disgusting. We have to take this to the headmaster."

"No, it's okay. I'll figure it out."

"Lorraine, this is a death threat." She shook the note at me. "They don't take these things lightly. He has a knife." Her voice rose an octave as she spoke.

I took the note back and tucked it into my pocket. "I know, but it's okay. Someone is just trying to scare me." It was too much to hope that she would know who did it, but it'd been worth the shot.

"Scare you? Well, then, it's working," she said. "On me anyway."

I pulled out my cell and dialed the phone my grandparents got that was reserved just for me. For my calls.

Crystal ignored the communication device at my ear.

"Maybe you're not scared, but trust me when I say fear has entered the building."

"You have reached a private number. Please leave a message." I soaked in the soothing sound of my grandmother's voice and waited for the beep.

"*I'm* scared."

Beep.

"Grandma, Granddad—," I began, but Crystal interrupted me.

"I mean, who wouldn't be scared?"

I shook my head and continued. "—something happened. Something changed."

"You act like this is nothing," she ranted.

"Call me back," I said into my phone. "Please."

"Like you get death threats every day."

I cupped my hand over the mic and whispered into the phone, "I need help."

Oblivious, Crystal stood and waved her arms about wildly. "We need to get the authorities involved."

With disappointment consuming me, I hung up. I really wanted to talk to them. To hear their reassurances that everything would be okay.

"We need to call the cops. Our state senators." She pointed her index finger toward the heavens. "The White House!"

But mostly, I wanted to go home.

Crystal frowned. "These kinds of things should not be allowed to happen in our schools."

I shouldn't have left my family and friends. I should never have run.

"We are the future."

Apparently, if I die, everyone dies. Cleary my destiny was not something I could outrun. If I could survive the next few days, maybe it wasn't too late. Maybe I could still do what I was supposed to be doing, whatever that entailed, to try to stop the coming war.

"What time is it?" I asked her for no reason whatsoever as I checked my phone.

"Our safety should be guaranteed," she replied.

Almost four. Crap on a cracker. I'd been sleeping for over two hours. Classes would be over and the halls would be empty. "Do you know any bodyguards who might see us to our room?" I asked her.

She stared at me, her jaw set, her shoulders square. "Safety is not a privilege. It is our right as law-abiding, taxpaying citizens!"

AIM HERE

I was beginning to regret my decision to show Crystal the note as we headed back to the dorm rooms. I had to think. To plan. If someone was going to kill me, I needed to know who. And how to stop him. And Crystal's ranting about our constitutional rights was not helping, no matter how entertaining.

A sickly weakness spread throughout my body as though I were a doe in the forest, standing in the crosshairs of a hunter's rifle, only it was night and I had a neon sign on my back that read AIM HERE. Picasso knew who I was, but I had no clue who he was. The kid who left the note was just that. A kid. Like every other kid who went to Bedford Fields. If he'd been different, if he hadn't belonged here, wouldn't others have turned to look at him as he walked past? All I saw was the back of his head, but no one spared him a glance. Then again, I could have been looking at the wrong head.

Vulnerability washed over me again. A neon target. That was me.

We'd left the nurse's office without telling her. Mostly because she'd been in and out all afternoon, and when we left, she was out. But surely she didn't mean for me to lie there all evening. The halls were empty save for a custodian on the second floor. I almost asked him to escort us back to our dorm but thought better of it. He might have to tell the headmaster. I was a tad intimated by the headmaster and wanted to avoid contact with him as much as possible.

"Oh, some people came by to see you," Crystal said, carving some time out of her busy rant schedule to let me know. "A couple."

"Really?" I asked, surprised, then realized it must have been the Hamptons, the couple who'd brought me here. Dropped me off at the school. Told me to find their son, Paul. Promised he'd keep an eye out for me, too, but in my entire six weeks at the stuffy institution, I had yet to meet a kid named Paul.

I hadn't asked any questions about him, either. At the time, I was numb. In shock. They'd been the last leg of the three-day journey across country that started in New Mexico and ended in Maine. I'd wanted nothing more than to turn around and go back home. But my despair wasn't their fault. They were part of the Order of Sanctity, a group that followed and believed in the teachings and prophecies of Arabeth and her descendants. They were believers. In me and my part in all of this, the part I was destined to play in the end times.

When they first laid eyes on me, they seemed starstruck. They'd been hearing about me since my birth, the first female to be born in the line of Arabeth's descendants in over five centuries. Apparently my birth meant the prophecies were coming true, the end of times was growing near, but their reverence made me uncomfortable. It prickled down my spine. In a way, I felt bad for them. Sorry. And my sorrow was full of resentment and anger. I'd had to leave everything I'd ever known, ever loved, for these people and others like them. Because they believed in me. What a crock.

But when I looked at things from their vantage point, I could almost understand their reverence in a small, vexatious way. In their world, I was like a rock star, the subject of all those prophecies that had been passed down from generation to generation. I tried to see things from their point of view. And in the day I'd spent with them, I grew to like the Hamptons very much. They were a young couple—too young to have a kid in high school, in my limited opinion—and they were full of ideas on how they were going to change the world. After I saved it, naturally.

They meant well, and I did my best to stow my doubts and try to appreciate all that they were doing for me. It wasn't their fault any more than it was mine. We'd all been dragged into a catastrophic chain of events that would either end humanity or restore the balance. If that outcome depended on me, we were all in a world of trouble. I wasn't nearly so confident in our odds as the Hamptons were.

After they showed me into the headmaster's office the

night we arrived, Mrs. Hampton pulled me into her arms and hugged me as though I were her own child, and I was beginning to see a pattern. All the people along the journey treated me similarly. As though I were theirs. I realized they probably saw me that way. They'd heard about me for years. Had hoped for me even longer. How could I resent that? How could I throw their hope back at them and rant and scream and pout? Their faith in me was humbling, their faith in God inspirational. I decided to see it as a benefit instead of a burden.

"Hey, do you know a Paul Hampton?" I asked Crystal. "I was supposed to keep an eye out for him."

"Not really. What grade is he in?"

I tended to forget Crystal was only in the eighth grade. She wouldn't have any classes with Paul. Then again, I had no idea what grade Paul was in. "You know, I'm not sure. I just assumed he was older, but I never actually asked."

"We can ask Wade at dinner," she offered.

"Ask Wade what?"

We turned to see Wade jogging up behind us. He was my only other friend at Bedford Fields. He was a nice kid. One of the few who stayed nice after my shiny newness wore off. His dark hair fell into disarray as he stopped beside us.

Crystal obliged him. "If you know a Paul Hampton."

His forehead crinkled. "Sure I do. Everyone does. He's been coming to school here forever."

"Oh," she said. "I guess I just missed him."

His dark gaze landed on me along with a playful grin. "Where you been? You missed Mr. Parton's lecture on how *not* to write a five-page essay."

"No way." I rolled my eyes. "I can't believe I missed it. I'd been so looking forward to the lecture."

"It's the talk of the town," he said. He took an apple out of his backpack and took a huge bite. "Okay, I'm out of here. Gotta change out of this crap before dinner."

Dinner was one of the few places we could appear at the school out of uniform, but we still had strict guidelines to follow, so even there everyone dressed way too nice for my peace of mind. I just stuck to my uniform. I saw what happened to students who didn't follow the guidelines. They were immediately singled out and escorted to the headmaster's office. I'd rather die from a thousand ant bites than be singled out in a room full of rich kids with nothing better to do than laugh at me.

"I wonder what we're having tonight," Crystal said, referring to what awaited us in the dining hall later as Wade jogged off. I fought the urge to call him back. He didn't need to know about the notes I'd been getting, the death threats. But it would have been nice to have him close.

"Oh, I hope it's pizza with shrimp," she said as we started for our room again. "I love pizza with shrimp."

There were two very cool things I was learning about Maine. One, the landscape was incredible. It was gorgeous and had shades of green I'd never seen before. Two, the food was amazing. I'd never had so much seafood in my life, and I loved it. Seafood in Riley's Switch was canned tuna on rye.

I started to almost feel normal again, talking about food and dreaming about landscapes, when we turned a corner and ran into my newest archnemesis.

"Hey, Pratt," Kenya said. She was leaning against a wall, checking out her black nail polish. For the first time since I'd arrived at BFA, her presence was welcome and oddly comforting. At least with two other people around, the odds of someone stabbing me to death diminished.

I straightened and feigned normalcy as I walked past, praying she'd follow. Praying she'd torment. "Hey, Kenya. It's too bad about your hair."

She didn't care in the least what I thought about her hair, which had been bleached so many times, it had the same texture as that fake spider webbing they sold at Halloween. She smirked and fell in line behind us.

I pocketed a relieved smile.

"You seem pale," she said, matching our strides.

Crystal glared over her shoulder and wrapped an arm in mine. I'd veered to the left a little, the ground tilting beneath my feet.

"I'm fine," I said when I'd regained my balance. "You're not worried about me, are you?"

She snorted. "Not likely. But I have to admit to a certain amount of curiosity about you."

"And why would you be curious about someone like me?"

"Exactly. Which makes it all the more curious."

The minute I got to my dorm room, I tore through my drawers, looking for a weapon, anything I could use to defend myself. Crystal sat atop her bed and watched me. I reconsidered my refusal to take the note to the headmaster like Crystal said for about five seconds before coming to my senses. That would only draw attention. I was here to be incognito, keep to the shadows, not focus a spotlight on myself.

I tried my grandparents again, but got the voice mail for the third time. Which was beyond strange. They always carried that phone. At least one of them had it on their person at all times, day and night. Receiving no answer, I gave up on the whole incognito thing and tried their regular cell phones. Nothing. Then the store landline. Nothing again.

I grew more worried by the minute. Should I try Brooklyn? Glitch? Maybe the church?

No one but my grandparents knew where I was. How would I explain everything to my best friends if I were to call them? Would they be happy to hear from me? Angry I'd run? I just couldn't imagine, though I'd enacted our reunion a thousand times in my head. Brooklyn and I would see each other from across a field of green grass. She would run to me with open arms. Glitch would do the same, only he'd trip on something—quite possibly air—and spill his whipped almond toffee cappuccino with nonfat milk all over my flowing white dress, the one I'd bought for running across a field during my homecoming. Cameron would stand to the side and scowl like we were all crazy and he regretted ever meeting us. And Jared . . .

Jared would smile. He would cross his arms while waiting for my best friends to get their greetings out of the way, and then he'd walk forward, pull me into his arms, lower his head—

"Lorraine!"

I snapped back to the present and blinked at Crystal.

"I've got it!" she said, her wide eyes full of enthusiasm. "We can put the note in the headmaster's office and pretend like it was sent to *him*."

"Oh, that wouldn't get us expelled. And, more than likely, arrested."

"No, it's perfect. If there's a death threat against the headmaster, the authorities will use all their resources to find out who sent it."

"Exactly. Jail time. For us."

She rolled her eyes right before I dived under my bed for the canvas bag I'd brought with me from home.

"No, they'll check the paper for fingerprints and stuff."

I grabbed the bag and popped back up to question her. "Fingerprints like ours?"

"No. Oh, wait. Yes. Never mind."

She exhaled, blowing her bangs out of her eyes before falling back in frustration.

After a thorough check of my bag, I gave up finding a weapon of any kind among my possessions. I just didn't think Picasso would be intimidated by a hairbrush. Or a toothbrush. Then again, I could sharpen the tip like they did in prison. Make a shank out of it.

"Do you know how to make a shank?" I asked Crystal. I'd given up on my things and had started rummaging around hers instead.

She rolled onto her side, propped her head up, and watched me. "Sure, I guess. We'll need soap, a lighter, and an old comb."

I paused. "What movie did you get that from?"

"Movie?" She frowned in thought. "I used to do it when I was a kid. The trick is getting the mold just right. I can make a wicked shank with a serrated blade and a dragon emblem, given enough time. And, well, soap."

My admiration of her just increased tenfold. "You're kind of amazing," I said.

She looked as though she didn't understand, like I'd spoken a foreign language. "Thank you," she replied after a solid minute. "No one's ever said that to me."

I bounced up. "That's a tragedy, because it's true. I'm going to the dining room early to lift a knife."

"Okay. Want me to come?"

"No, I don't want to get you in trouble for stealing."

She jumped up. "But I can help. I can be your lookout."

Crystal had a bright future ahead of her, and as much as I wanted the company, I didn't want to get her expelled. Or stabbed repeatedly, should Picasso show up. "I'll be okay. You stay here and try to come up with another plan on how we can figure out who this guy is without garnering prison sentences."

"But I think much better on my feet."

"Crystal—"

"And you're not getting rid of me that easily." She jammed her fists onto her hips, her mind made up.

"Okay, but if you miss out on Harvard because of your time in juvie, don't come crying to me."

"Harvard?" she asked, aghast. "I'm shooting for Stanford. San Francisco is calling my name."

"Nice. Is it saying, 'Hey, crazy little girl. Want some candy?'"

"How did you know?" she asked, her eyes twinkling with humor.

I laughed as we hurried out of our room. Dinner was not for another hour, but hopefully the doors would be unlocked anyway. Surely they'd have a knife I could carry for self-defense. But the minute I stepped out of my room, I came face-to-face with Kenya. Again. What was with her?

A niggling of recognition registered in the deepest, darkest corners of my mind. I'd been followed before. And, similarly, it was by someone who was not particularly fond of me at the time. Cameron Lusk.

Kenya was acting very much like Cameron might. Shady. Secretive. Volatile. Only Cameron, I found out later, had been following me to protect me. Not to kick my ass. Still, she carried a switchblade. She had a weapon and seemed to know how to use it. I couldn't decide if that was a good thing or not, but as long as she was dead set on tormenting me any-way, she may as well be of some use.

While I would normally be encouraging her to find a better use of her time, suggesting she take up belly dancing or parachute-less skydiving, for once I wanted her close. Of course, I couldn't let her know that, so I played the part of hapless victim.

"Don't you have somewhere else to be?" I asked, letting a touch of frustration filter into my voice. "I heard there's some third-graders who still have their milk money. If you hurry . . ."

Crystal nodded in agreement, then added, "Or you could go rob a liquor store. I hear there's a bright future in that."

I flashed Crystal a surprised smile. She was pretty good at this stuff.

"Or," Kenya said, her voice just as controlled as mine, just as bored, "I could wait until you two are alone and stab you both to death."

I stopped and turned to her.

She stopped, too, and probed me with a questioning gaze. "What?" she said, but she seemed wary, suspicious.

Could it have been her? Did she put the note in my pocket? I thought it was that boy, but who knows when the note was deposited? Maybe Kenya put it there earlier and I simply didn't notice until I was in the bathroom, throwing up my latest meal.

"Was it you?" I asked, astonished she'd go that far with her idle threats. Then again, maybe they weren't as idle as I thought.

She grabbed hold of my arm and pulled me toward her. "Was what me? What happened?"

I jerked out of her grip. The last thing I wanted to see was her death again, not that I'd ever had the same vision twice. Once usually did the trick. But just in case, I stepped away from her just as Crystal slid in between us.

"Go away," she said, standing up to the playground bully with the bravado of an eccentric pirate. "Go find your own kind or something."

Kenya's gaze slid past her and narrowed on me, her thick liner making her look more menacing than she normally would. "It's a free country. I can hang out here if I want to."

"Whatever," I said, continuing toward the dining room.

But we didn't shake her. Kenya stayed right behind us. Surely she wouldn't stab me in front of a witness, if that was her goal. But why? I wanted to look at the note again, but didn't dare pull it out in front of Kenya. I'd just assumed it was a boy, but I could've been wrong. Maybe the note had a clue that I'd missed, one that would let me know the gender of my attacker. It would have to wait, however, with the switchblade stalker fast on our heels.

I also wanted to try my grandparents again. Something was wrong. I could feel it. But again, I didn't dare talk to them in front of Kenya. The less she knew about me, the better.

We hurried down the stairs and out the front door toward the dining hall. Everyone we passed glanced at me sideways. Smirked a little.

"Oh, my gosh," Crystal said, checking her phone.

"What?" I asked, keeping most of my attention focused on our blond-haired shadow. "Did you solve the mysteries of antimatter?"

"No. Nothing." She turned off her phone and stuffed it into her jacket pocket.

Oh, like that wouldn't spike my curiosity. "Crystal, you are

the worst liar in school. What?" I asked as we slogged over
the damp grounds.

She pulled her lower lip through her teeth, before saying,
"No, really, it's nothing. Someone posted a picture in the
school news feed. People are dumb."

I raised my brows at her and waited for her to cave. She
really was the worst liar. And she had no stamina. She caved
immediately.

"Okay," she said in a hushed tone. She pulled her phone
back out, shielding it from our stalker. "But just remember,
people are dumb."

I chuckled. "Got it. People are dumb."

She brought up her Friendbook feed and scrolled down
to a photo someone had posted earlier that day. I squinted
and looked closer. It was a group of kids. Bedford Fields
kids. In the exact hallway we'd left earlier. And, yep. There
I was. Falling on my butt in front of man and beast alike.

A kid named Zach-Z had snapped a shot of me when I
had the rush of visions in the hall. What a great guy. I'm sure
he was only thinking of my well-being.

Wait. A picture. I blinked and looked at it again.

I had a picture!

I almost tripped as I scrambled to get my own phone out.
Suddenly all the sideways smirks made sense. No doubt
everyone in school had seen it. The image already had hundreds of likes. Wonderful. Just what my social life needed.
But at least I had something I could work with.

The dining room was open, but dinner wasn't being served
yet. We sat at our usual table, which was about fifty miles
south of the cool table. It was easy to spot, thus easy to avoid.
I glanced behind us, and Kenya was gone. I did a 360. Yep,
she was gone. There were a few kids lingering as well. We

weren't really supposed to be in here yet, but until we got kicked out, we were going to stay.

"Do you see a knife?" I asked Crystal.

She lowered her head as though disappointed.

"What?"

"I thought we were going to make one."

Fighting a grin, I said, "We can, but later. Right now I just need some small semblance of protection."

"You're right. Sorry." She scanned the room. "There's a cheese knife on the sideboard."

"It's better than nothing, I guess. I was kind of hoping for a paring knife. Something small but really sharp."

"That makes sense." She waved as Wade walked up to us.

"What are you guys doing here?"

He'd changed out of his school uniform into civvies. That's what the students called regular clothes. At first, I thought the idea of going to a school with uniforms would be cool, but it got old kind of fast. The pants and skirts were pleated. Very old school. I had only two sets, so I had to do laundry often.

"We're on a mission," Crystal said to Wade.

"Seriously?" He leaned in, intrigued. Wade was a lifer, as he liked to call himself. He'd been going to Bedford Fields since he was in preschool. He'd never known anything else. And even though his parents lived close by, he chose to start living at the school when he was in seventh.

His dark hair hung in its usual disarray. Crystal chatted with him as I studied the picture Zach-Z had posted.

"We need a knife," she said. "For personal protection."

I was hoping she wouldn't mention the note and she didn't.

"A knife? So you come to the dining room?"

"Yes." Her hackles rose at his tone. "Where else do you suppose we get a knife?"

As they discussed the best places close by to pick up a knife that could be easily concealed yet deadly when needed, I put my fingers on my phone, ran my fingertips along the cool glass. Hopefully this would be a quick trip, I thought as I dived inside.

After the pixels merged into one solid picture, the first thing that hit me was the soft roar of conversation in the hallways. The gray color of both the walls and the uniforms, each with navy blue accents. I saw myself as I ran first into Kenya, then into a boy. I stumbled but managed to gain my footing just as another kid brushed past me and I lost all the ground I'd gained.

I could see the visions as they coursed through me, pummeled me like a wrecking ball until I crumbled and slid to the ground. I covered my mouth as bile slipped up the back of my throat. I tripped trying to get to the bathroom. I started to fall, and the replay ended.

"Don't you agree?" Crystal said.

After drawing in a shaky breath, I said, "I'm sorry. What?"

"Don't you think we should go tonight? We can't leave campus after seven. We should just go and grab something to eat on the way."

It was always weird seeing myself from a different vantage. Watching myself from a distance. And this was no exception. I could see the shock wave rush through me when each vision hit. I could see myself turning blue as death after death played out before my eyes. I could see the fear that they felt on my own face, could see their despair and suffering in my expression as it flashed through me like a nuclear blast. But I'd felt the tug on my coat earlier. Before this.

I needed to go further back in the picture. I needed to rewind the scene just a few minutes more. But to when?

"Okay," I said, trying to appease her.

Crystal had been there when I felt the tug. I had to try to manipulate time to see further back. I bit down and concentrated.

"So, now?" Crystal asked.

I gave them a blank stare. "What?"

"The knife. The weapon. We should go now before curfew."

"Oh, no, I can't go," I said, blinking back to them. "I don't have any money."

I did have money, actually, a little, but I couldn't waste it. I was saving it for a plane ticket. I had a feeling I was going to be rushing back home. If I was going to die in the apocalypse, I was going to do it among family and friends.

"I do," Wade said. "My parents are loaded."

I smiled. "I can't take your money."

"Not mine," he corrected. "My parents'."

My smile morphed into a teasing glare. "I can't take your parents' money either."

"Come on," he said, pulling at my jacket sleeve. "It'll be fun. Just the three of us."

When he tugged my sleeve, his fingers brushed across the back of my hand. I'd been diving into pictures, my mind focused, so I'd left myself wide open again. I got a vision before I could brace against one. Before I could erect my mental barrier.

I bit down, braced myself, expecting to be shown Wade's death. Usually when I had a vision, I was shown the most pressing issue for that person. An imminent death. A wreck that damaged a spine. The loss of a loved one. But it was different with Wade. Darker. Hungrier.

Gone was his sweet, easygoing nature. A predator had emerged. With my fingers still on the screen, I was first catapulted back into the picture. I watched as Wade watched me. Followed me. Waited until I was so crushed by students, I wouldn't notice him as he slipped the note into my pocket. His hands shook when he drew it, but not with fear or anxiety. With anger. With a seething kind of hatred.

He hurried through the throngs after depositing the note, then waited for the halls to clear, hoping to catch me looking at it. But I'd fallen, like the stupid bitch I was. He curled his hands into fists, frustrated he didn't get to see the look on my face when I saw his masterpiece.

That was okay. He'd see the shock on it when his knife punctured my heart. When he stole the beast within me. Surely when I died, the beast would leave the vessel it was in and search out another. And he'd be there waiting. With that thing inside him, he'd be strong. Invincible.

First thing he'd do? Kill his parents.

No, wait. First he'd kill Headmaster Tompkins. He'd cut his face with a broken bottle and watch him bleed out.

Of course, before he could do any of that, he'd have to kill the prophet. The great prophet who was going to save the world.

The thought of putting a stop to that nonsense made him hardened. Every time he realized the prophet he'd heard about his entire, miserable life had practically fallen into his lap, he wanted to laugh with glee. It was a gift from heaven. Or would have been if he believed in heaven. After growing up with parents as loony as the day was long, he wasn't sure heaven existed anymore.

Still, they'd been right about the prophet. They were believers. They'd taught him about her since he was a kid. They'd longed to meet her, to invite her to stay with them, to call her their own. They never said that, of course, but he could see it in their eyes every time they looked at him. Their disappointment. Their desire for something more in their child. Something that hinted at greatness.

He'd show them greatness. Right before he pulled the trigger, he'd show them just how great he could be . . . with a demon inside him.

If only Lorelei weren't so freaking stupid. How could this idiot girl from a bass-ackward state like New Mexico, of all places, end up being the prophet? How could she have such exquisite power lurking just beneath her skin and not utilize it? He wanted to bash her skull in with a baseball bat every time he thought about it.

"Lorraine?"

I heard Crystal's voice through the fog of hatred and venom. Shock held me down longer than I would've liked, but I eventually clawed my way to the surface, following Crystal's voice out of the vortex Wade had sent me to.

He still had his hand on my jacket sleeve, a silicon smile painted onto his face.

I jerked my hand back and a hint of suspicion flitted across his eyes. Not only did he know I was the prophet, but he knew my real name as well. He'd thought it in my vision. How? Who were his parents?

"What do you think?" Crystal asked. "I can pitch in, too. I've been saving my money for a rainy day, and guess what? It's raining! No, really. I heard it."

Wade's eyes didn't leave mine, his expression knowing, accepting.

"Come on," he urged again. "We'll find you a knife. Everyone needs protection in this day and age. Even our schools aren't safe."

"I just told her that!" Crystal shouted, thrilled that someone was agreeing with her. "I think we need to write the governor. This is just ridiculous. Our security measures are way too lax."

"I agree," he said. He didn't move an inch. He watched me, took in my every move, calculated how hard it would be to push the knife he had hidden in his coat through my sternum and into my heart. Or that was where my mind was headed. My thoughts.

Who would I go to? I couldn't tell the headmaster. The police. Who would believe me?

How much should I bring out into the open? How much should I reveal to Wade? Should I tell him I knew everything? Would that dissuade him? Divert him from his current path? Or would that just rev up his plans? Throw him into overdrive? Get myself killed even faster?

"I'm not hungry," I said to Crystal, scooting my chair back from the table.

Wade straightened, his suspicions causing the barest hint of a grin to twitch the corners of his mouth.

"Do you feel bad again?" she asked me, alarmed.

"Yes, I do. I'm sorry." I started to rise, but I could hardly leave Crystal alone with a bona fide psychopath. She needed to know who he was. What he was. And she needed to steer all kinds of clear of this guy. What a whack job.

Then again, how did I explain this to her? My position was too precarious. Too much was at stake for me to risk anything. I had to survive the next few days. I had to at least try to stop the coming war.

Left with little choice, I realized I had to leave. Now. I could hardly fight him. A knife in even the most inept hands was a very dangerous weapon. It wasn't like I knew karate. Or judo. Or Pilates. I totally should have watched more Bruce

Lee movies growing up. Considering my lack of experience, I didn't stand a chance against him. He seemed quite determined. And agile.

I'd made up my mind. Tonight I would sneak out, buy a plane ticket, and go home.

WITNESS PROTECTION

I took Crystal's arm and dragged her behind me. Wade nodded a good-bye as we left, biding his time, I supposed. The halls were beginning to fill with students filtering toward the dining hall. He couldn't very well stab me there, not without expecting some serious prison time.

"Are you sure you're okay?" Crystal asked me for the seventh time.

I thrust her inside our room, then started tearing through it again, realizing in my haste I'd forgotten to get a weapon.

Wonderful. First I changed into civvies; then I started throwing things into my canvas bag, not worrying about my uniforms. I needed to travel light. I was busy picking out my essentials like hair gel and toothpaste when a knock sounded at the door.

Crystal had been talking, but she stopped and looked at me. "Should I answer it?"

I slammed my eyes shut when I noticed I hadn't locked it. Of all the boneheaded things not to do. Holding up a hand to her, I tiptoed over and turned the bolt. The lock slid into place before I asked, "Who is it?"

"It's Kenya. You dropped your phone."

I gasped and tore through the pockets of my school jacket. It was gone. I was just about to open the door when another thought hit. Maybe they were working together. Didn't she just talk about stabbing me to death? How could she have known that?

"Just leave it by the door. I think I have a stomach virus. I don't want to get you sick."

Crystal gave me a thumbs-up for my quick thinking. We waited. I pressed my ear to the door, hoping to hear retreating footsteps. Instead, I heard the bolt on my door turn. Before I could relock it, Kenya crashed through the door. I stumbled back but caught myself fast. Not that it would help. Like Wade, she also carried a knife. I was beginning to see Crystal's point about our security measures being a tad lax.

"What are you doing?" Kenya asked, taking in the disarray of our room.

"How did you open my door?"

She showed me a key. A master key like the custodians used. Perfect. "Again, what are you doing?"

"Laundry," I said. "Can I just have my phone?"

My stomach churned, so if Kenya pushed it, I was pretty sure I could prove to her I felt nauseated.

She tossed the phone to me, closed the door behind her, then strolled over and sat on top of my desk like she owned the world.

"What are you doing?" I asked her, fear causing a line of sweat under my nose and over my brows.

She took out her switchblade and pointed to my surroundings. "What are you doing?"

"I already told you." I spotted the note on the desk beside her and looked away quickly. Too quickly.

She picked it up, opened it, and studied it for several tense heartbeats. Did she know about it? Was she in on the whole thing? I didn't see her in my vision of Wade, but I rarely got a whole picture.

"Interesting artwork," she said, folding it and placing it back where she found it. She pulled her bottom lip through her teeth, then as abruptly as a lightning burst, jumped off the desk and strolled out of the room. Right before she closed the door, she turned to me and said, "Do not leave this room." Then she slammed the door.

What? Was I supposed to sit there and wait for her to come back and knife me? Not even.

"Holy crap, lock the door!" she yelled from the hallway.

I rushed forward and locked it. Not that it would help.

I turned to Crystal. "How did she get a master key?"

Her eyes were wide when she lifted her shoulders.

"Well, I have to finish packing." I dived into my work again, sorting through my things. I brought way more than I'd thought.

"I still don't get why you're leaving," she said.

I seemed to be hurting her feelings. "I have to get home.

Back to New Mexico ay-sap. My grandmother called and my grandfather is in the hospital."

I didn't want to tell her too much too soon. If Wade thought she knew something, she could be in danger. I'd explain to her once I was gone. Once the danger of having me around had passed.

I didn't want to call a cab from the school. It would look bad having one pull up in the middle of the night after curfew. I was certain the headmaster would be called. So, I packed up what I could, left Crystal my favorite pillow and a bracelet I'd bought on the trip over. It had the shape of New Mexico on it.

"Why New Mexico?" she asked, and I realized my mistake too late. I was supposed to be from Arizona.

After throwing my bag over my shoulder, grabbing my purse and phone, and stuffing the death threat into my pocket, I stood before her and said, "My name is really Lorelei McAlister. I'm from New Mexico, not Arizona. The rest I'll have to explain to you once I'm away, once you're safe."

"Are you in the Witness Protection Program?" she asked, her lashes fluttering like butterfly wings.

"Yes," I said, lying like a dehydrated dog in July. "Yes, I am."

She swore not to tell anyone. Ever. As long as she lived.

I put my hand on her arm. "Thank you. My family's lives depend on it."

I was going to hell.

I hefted my canvas bag with all my worldly possessions onto my hip. The strap was already cutting into my shoulder and I hadn't even gotten past the campus grounds yet. The darkness left all kinds of shadows hovering around me, thick and menacing. Anyone could be waiting in them. Anyone could ambush me without a moment's notice. I suddenly realized how utterly stupid my plan was. I should've called a cab regardless. What would the headmaster do? There was nothing he could do. It wasn't like they had my real name. Once I left the school grounds, how would they find me?

There was a twenty-four-hour café down the street. I just had to get past the guard posted at the entrance; then I could wait in there for the cab. And have some coffee to warm up.

At least one part of my plan made sense. I would be gone before Wade the psychotic stick boy, according to his own drawing, figured it out. He wouldn't have a chance to kill me. I stopped as another thought surfaced. Would he retaliate? Would he go after Crystal? The headmaster? His parents?

I should have warned her, I thought as I shivered in the cold. It bit into my bones, clamping on, locking its jaws like a pit bull the moment I stepped out into the frigid night air. A thick fog circled around me, the haze creating a halo effect that I could see only in the low light of the lamps that lit the pathways from the academic buildings to the dorms, through the maintenance buildings, and across to the guardhouse.

That would be the real trick, getting past that house.

The aloneness I suddenly felt weighed heavily. I wrapped my fingers tighter around the strap of my bag, and it occurred to me that I'd never lifted a knife from the kitchen. I had nothing with which to defend myself should it come to that. What if Wade was watching? What if he stabbed me before I even saw him coming? Then again, maybe he had other plans. The picture he'd drawn showed a knife, but he could have anything. A gun. An axe. A hammer.

I quickened my footsteps. Every dark machination I could think of came to mind. My plan, if one could even call it that, seemed less and less favorable by the second. I would have to pass through some pretty dark nooks and crannies to get off grounds, but Wade hadn't come after me yet. Surely he didn't suspect I'd do something like this.

The gates to the grounds loomed near, as did the guard-house. Thirty feet ahead. On one hand, I had to somehow sneak past it. On the other, if Wade came after me now, I could call out to the guard.

Twenty feet.

I thought about the fact that I would soon be on a plane headed home. The feeling gave me that extra push I needed to plod onward. I could do this.

Ten feet.

I patted my jacket pocket, where I'd stashed my money. It would be enough for a ticket. It had to be. I didn't have time to take a bus. I needed to get back fast. The world was about to end.

I began to tiptoe as I got closer to the guardhouse. The gate beyond it was closed, but I was not above climbing over the fence and hurling my body into the darkness on the other side. With infinite care, I inched up to the lit guard-house and peeked in. No one was in it. All that worry for nothing.

The night guard was probably making rounds or some-thing. I had no idea, really, but it sounded logical that part of his job would be to make rounds. With fate smiling upon me, I hurried to the shadows of the fence beside the gate. I could never have climbed up the gate itself. It was a massive iron thing with long, menacing bars. Much like a jail cell. There was nothing to grab on to, and the tops of the bars were sharp and pointy. I would impale myself if I even attempted it. They would find my lifeless body the next morning, dangling from a spike.

Why I had to think such things at a time like this was beyond me. Crystal told me she'd heard about kids climbing over the fence using the hinges for leverage. I tried to throw my bag over first, but I couldn't quite get the distance I needed. That fence was at least fifteen feet high. I managed about three. Possibly four. And it hurt when it came back down. So I threw it back over my shoulder and proceeded to climb. Or, I thought about climbing until I heard a snicker in the dark beside me.

My foot slipped and I almost fell before I turned around and saw a male figure standing off to the side, his silhouette actually a little lighter than the shadow he was in. This was not happening. Surely Wade didn't follow me. But when the boy slid from the shadows, I realized that trying to outrun fate was a lot harder than it sounded.

Wade did indeed stand before me, his arms crossed over his chest, a smug grin tainting his face. He was suddenly ugly. I didn't remember him being ugly before, but he seemed that way to me now.

A healthy dose of adrenaline dumped into my central nervous system and swept through my body. The first expression to rush across my face, the one that escaped before I could catch it, was fear. Panic. I immediately reined that in and let a look of mild disinterest settle in its place.

Time to make a new friend.

"Do you mind?" I asked, gesturing toward the guardhouse. I went to step around him, but he matched my step, staying locked between me and safety. I prayed he didn't know the guard wasn't there and forced my poker face to stay put. No sense in letting him see how scared I was. How my insides were churning with terror. If I knew anything about people who preyed on what they saw as a weaker specimen of the species, it was that they liked to see the fear on their victims' faces. They liked to hear it in their thundering heartbeats and their quivering voices.

So I schooled my expression to stay neutral, stopped, and offered him my best look of bored annoyance, the one I'd most recently learned from Kenya.

"Are we going to do this all day?" I asked. "Because I have places to be."

"Looks like it." He surveyed the fence I was just about to climb. Or attempt to climb. No idea if I would have succeeded, and now I'd never know.

I sighed to emphasize how boring I found him. "Are you going to turn me in or what? If so, let's get on with it. Like I said, I have places to be."

I sidestepped again before spotting the glint of light off a blade in his hands.

"This won't take long," he assured me.

Fear gripped me so hard, my lungs struggled under the weight of it. If I died, would everyone die? Was it really that cut and dried? That ridiculously simple? Surely God wouldn't let that happen. Surely the fate of the world didn't rest on the condition of my heart. But I'd seen it with my own eyes. The deaths of hundreds of thousands of people. Possibly millions. It was like a switch had been flipped and I didn't know how to unflip it.

He took a menacing step closer.

"The guard is right there," I said, gesturing with a nod.

Wade laughed softly. "Don't worry. He won't be bothering anyone for a very long time."

I gasped and dropped my bag with every intention of running toward the guardhouse to check on the man. Was he in it? Did Wade hurt him? After reading his emotions in my vision, I wouldn't put it past him.

But Wade stepped in my path once again. And getting closer to him would put me that much closer to the knife.

"You are all I've heard about my whole life," he said, his tone suddenly angry, his words taut. Forced. "Growing up, my parents didn't brag about me, but you. The last prophet. Hallelujah, the last prophet had been born at last!" He raised his hands in the air and waved them, mocking churchgoers everywhere. "The girl who's going to save the world." He leveled his cold stare on me again. "They thought I wasn't listening," he said, tapping the knife against his leg. "I was."

"Prophet?" I said, projecting the best look of absurdity in my arsenal. "I have no idea what you're talking about."

He lowered his head and glared at me from underneath his lashes. "If you lie to me again, I'll draw this out as long as I can."

"You have the wrong perso—"

He held up a finger. "Before you go there, I just want you to know, I only want what's inside you. You I don't care about in the least. You can either die quick and painlessly, or slow and, well, with lots and lots of pain."

His words caused my throat to cinch shut. My pulse raced, barreling toward the finish line, apparently. "Just because you're disillusioned doesn't mean you have to kill me."

"Disillusioned?" He acted insulted. "Do you have any idea what it's been like growing up in the shadow of a girl you've never even met? Who your parents had never even met?"

His parents? How did his parents know about me? "Let's say I am who you think I am. I am this prophet. How did you know?"

"I told you." He kicked the dirt at his feet in anger. "My parents have been raving about you since I was a kid."

"Who are your parents? Are they members of the Order?"

"Members?" he scoffed. "More like worshippers of the great Lorelei McAlister. You should have seen them when they got the call." He spit into the darkness at his side, his features twisted into a fanatical rage. "They were going to get to drive you here. To keep watch over you while you were here."

My jaw fell open in surprise. "The Hamptons? Your parents are the nice couple who drove me here?"

"Nice? Did you get a sense of how much they worship you when they picked you up?"

I did, actually, but I wasn't about to tell him that.

"You're Paul?"

He spread his arms wide, the knife in his right hand gleaming in the moonlight. "The one and only. What'd they tell you? To search me out? That I'd keep an eye on you?" He laughed softly. "Trust me, I did. I never took my eyes off you."

How did such a nice couple have such a psychotic son?

He was so angry. I had to get through to him somehow. Perhaps a little honesty would go a long way. "Okay, you're right. I am who you think I am, and I have no idea what you've gone through, but let me explain something." I showed my palms in an act of surrender. "There is a war on the horizon. It is going to happen and it's going to happen soon. I've seen it. And it started the moment you put that note in my pocket."

He tilted his head, listening.

"Something changed when you did that. I have no idea why or what, but something changed."

"So, if you die," he said, filling in the pieces, "the world will end?"

"I don't know. Maybe. I'm not sure what the catalyst will be, but it's going to happen soon. I have to get back home. I have to figure this out."

"If you aren't the most arrogant thing. Won't my parents be disappointed."

"I'm not saying that. I have no idea what set the wheels in motion. I'm just saying that they are in motion. Now. As we speak."

"But if the demon inside you is inside me, then I can live through anything."

"Wade, it doesn't work like that. Humans can't survive a demon possession."

"Pfft, you did," he said as though I'd insulted him.

"Yes, and I don't know how. If you do this, Malak will kill you."

"Malak?" he said, his eyes glittering hungrily. "Its name is Malak?"

"Malak-Tuke, Lucifer's second-in-command. Or at least he used to be. And trust me, he is not something you want traipsing about your insides. He'll rip you apart."

"Then why didn't he rip you apart?"

Fair question. If only I knew. "We became fast friends," I said, having no idea what else to say. "But he's already made it clear to me he doesn't like you."

"Really?"

"Really."

"And how did he do that?"

"We have a connection. A bond. We think very much

alike, and since I'd like to rip you apart right now, I'm pretty sure he would, too."

"Unfortunately," he said, stepping closer, "that's a chance I'm willing to take."

There was going to be no reasoning with him. I was hoping that if we stood in the cold long enough, another guard would come or a student would pass by, but hope was dwindling by the second. He was getting impatient. My talk of Malak only whetted his appetite for the raw power the demon possessed. He was a fool, but most psychopaths were.

I decided to play off it, to keep him wanting more, keep him talking. I was shaking uncontrollably now, from both fear and the cold. "He's tall," I said as though reminiscing with a friend over ice cream. "As tall as the trees. His shoulders as wide as a building. And his claws are razor sharp. I've seen them slice open a chest in the blink of an eye."

Admittedly the one I'd seen slice open a chest was not the demon inside me. That happened in a vision I'd had before I'd actually met Jared, when he brushed up against me in a dark hallway. It was my only vision, in fact, involving the Angel of Death. In it, he fought a towering demon with a sword in a strange land with a desolate landscape, scorched clouds, and a roiling, violet sky.

I'd heard the clanging of metal after our arms touched in that narrow passageway and turned to watch in horror when the vision crashed into me. A boy no more than sixteen or seventeen, fierce and somehow not quite human, struggled with a dark, monstrous beast. The boy's arms corded as tendon and muscle strained against the weight of the sword he wielded. He slashed again and again, but the monster was fast, with razorlike talons and sharp, shimmering teeth, and the boy knew what those teeth felt like when they sank into flesh, knew the blinding pain that accompanied defeat. But he also knew the power he himself wielded, the raw strength that saturated every molecule of his body.

Another herculean effort landed in the monster's shoulder and continued through its thick chest. The monster sank under the boy's sword with a guttural scream. He looked on while the beast writhed in pain, watched it grow still as the life drained out of it, and somewhere in the back of the boy's mind, he allowed himself to register the burning of his lungs as he struggled to fill them with air.

Blood trickled between his fingers, down the length of his blade, and dripped to the powdery earth beneath his feet. I followed the trail of blood up to three huge gashes across his chest. Clearly the monster's claws had met their mark, laying the flesh of its enemy open. I gasped and covered my mouth with both hands as the boy spun toward me, sword at the ready. Squinting against the low sun, I could almost make out his features, but the vision evaporated before I got the chance. A heartbeat later, I was back in the dark hallway, gasping for air, one palm pressed against my temple, the other against the wall for balance.

And that had been my introduction to angels and demons. I met Jared later and recognized him from that vision, but it was so surreal, so impossible, I had a hard time believing what I'd seen. I thought it was a metaphor for something, like when one dreams and it really means something else. I found out later the vision did happen. It was as real as I was. As Wade was. As the knife was that he grasped so palpably close to me.

Wade stared, mesmerized. "How do you feel with it inside you?"

I shrugged. No need to start lying now. "I don't even know

he's there. I feel a ripple every once in a while, but that's about it."

Surprised, he asked, "Doesn't he make you feel more powerful? Able to do anything?"

"Wade, I can't do anything. With or without him, I'm just a human. He doesn't give me superpowers."

He sneered at me. "That's because you've never used what you have at your fingertips. I knew you were stupid, but come on. You have one of the most powerful beings in the universe inside you and he does nothing? Are you for real?"

"I'm for real, Wade. I'm no different with him than I was without."

"Then that makes you an idiot."

I wanted to scream at him. Perhaps I was going about this the wrong way. If he thought so highly of Malak-Tuke, then maybe I needed to let him believe his own words.

"Fine," I said, my shoulders deflating. "I'm trying to save your life here, Wade. You're right. You've been right all along. He'll protect me."

He stilled. Narrowed his eyes as though trying to decide if I was lying or not. No time like the present to see how my poker face measured up.

"If you try to hurt me in any way," I said, inching back, insulating myself with as much distance as I could get, "he'll rip out your jugular. You know, in case you were wondering."

He wanted to believe me in a way. He wanted to believe Malak was that powerful, that protective, but that would mean he couldn't kill me to get at him.

"It's a lose–lose proposition," I said, putting a few more inches between us. "If he won't protect me, then what makes you think he'll do that for you? If he will protect me, then you'll die trying to find out. Either way, you don't get to win this one, Wade. You just don't."

Anger shot through him visibly. He was torn. Neither scenario appealed to him, but one had to be true. There was no other option, and he knew it. He clenched his teeth and let a shout of frustration slip through them, punching his knees with his own fists. Unfortunately, he did not stab himself in the process.

"I guess I have to choose, then," he said after reining in his temper. He brought up the knife, swung it back and forth in a Z shape as though demonstrating how he was going to cut me. Showing me the pattern he planned to use. "And I gotta tell ya, McAlister, I've wanted you dead for a really long time."

How did I inspire such hatred in people I'd never even met?

We were far enough away from each other that I might manage a clean getaway. But I wasn't exactly a track star. My freedom wouldn't last long. Still, it would give me precious seconds to scream. Surely someone would hear.

I poised myself to run, bent my knees just enough to give me some leverage, when a girl stepped from the same shadows Wade had been hiding in. Dizzy with hope, I looked at him, trying not to let him know we had company just yet. Then I saw who it was and my heart sank.

No way. Kenya was with him? I closed my eyes against the disappointment. I was going to die so painfully.

No.

No, no, no.

I opened my eyes. If I was going to die, I was going to make them work for it.

A sudden surge of adrenaline catapulted me forward.

I attacked Wade, caught him off guard, but he quickly re-covered, using my own momentum to bring me to the ground and straddle me.

"You have spunk!" he shouted, his own adrenaline kick-ing in. "I like that."

He raised the knife, and our situation mimicked his pic-ture. Him straddling me. Stabbing me. And Kenya would stand back and enjoy the show.

Or so I thought.

I heard a sharp thud, then felt Wade go limp. He was toppling toward me when Kenya grabbed his wrist and kept the knife back protectively as he fell forward. I looked over his shoulder and realized she was holding a tree branch. She'd hit him.

We heard a male voice penetrate the darkness. "What's going on?"

Why would she do that?

"Over here!" Kenya shouted. "A student has been at-tacked."

A security guard ran up to us. "What happened?" he asked, but he didn't wait for an answer before calling for backup and telling the dispatcher on the other end to get the police.

When he was finished, Kenya helped him pull Wade off me.

"This guy attack you?" he asked, helping me up. His dark skin shimmered in the low light and I thought he was the most beautiful thing I'd ever seen. And he was really tall.

"Are you an angel, too?" I asked him.

Kenya glared at me.

"Not me, ma'am. Let's get you a seat."

"I think little Lorraine here hit her head when he knocked her to the ground," she said.

He took Wade's knife, then led me back to the guard-house and sat me on the concrete slab that surrounded it. Kenya sat beside me.

"Are you kidding me?" she whispered when he went to check on Wade. "What the hell was that?"

"What? He's really tall."

"No, that little stunt. You were like a cyclone with arms."

"He was going to kill me. I was going to get my punches in before he managed it."

"You looked right at me."

"I thought you were going to kill me, too."

She slapped a hand over her eyes. "For the love of gravy, McAlister, what did you think I was doing when I put my finger over my mouth to silence you?"

"I thought you were coming to kill me silently."

"I was sneaking up behind Wade," she said, replaying the incident with her index fingers. It was very helpful. And entertaining. "You know, all stealthy like. Then you go crazy and pull some kind of karate helicopter move. He could've killed you!"

She was shouting now. The guard turned back to us as he zip-tied Wade's hands behind his back.

"I don't understand," I said, shaking harder than I had been. I was so cold, I was losing the feeling in my lungs.

"Clearly," she said, rolling her eyes. "And now look at you. Holy cow."

She stood and went inside the guardhouse only to return with a blanket and a cup of water. At least I thought it was water. After draping the blanket over me, she handed me the cup, then sat back down. It was coffee. Steaming, scorching coffee, and it tasted like heaven.

Okay, it tasted like motor oil, but it felt like heaven.

"I can't take you anywhere," she said, utterly annoyed with me.

Before I could comment, the guard came back to us, cops pulled up with sirens blaring, and another guard was running across the grass toward us.

So much for sneaking out unnoticed.

A LOVE–HATE THING

I sat in the back of an ambulance still wrapped in the blanket Kenya found. She sat beside me, waiting for her parents to show up.

"I don't understand," I said to her as we watched the police interview the headmaster. He looked none too happy. This was very bad publicity for a school, so it was hard to blame him.

"What don't you get?" she asked.

"You hate me."

"I don't hate you, McAlister." She started playing with her nails, the black polish shimmering in the glaring light. "I didn't know how else to protect you."

My brows slid together as I watched her. "Protect me? And how do you know my name?"

One corner of her mouth tipped up to reveal a dimple. "I know who you are. My parents are members of the Order." The surprised look on my face made her giggle. "I knew who you were the moment you showed up. We'd been expecting you for days."

"We?" I asked.

"Me, Wade, and a couple others. We had no idea Wade would be the one I'd be protecting you from. Then again, he always was a douche."

Wade sat handcuffed in another ambulance. His anger when he woke up was astounding. I had no idea someone could turn so red. The guy wanted me dead. No doubt about it.

And then there was Kenya. "So you bully me?" I asked, appalled. "You threaten me every time I turn around?"

"I marked you as mine." She lifted a shoulder and let it fall as though what she'd done was everyday. Normal. Ordinary. "No one else would bother you as long as you were my mark. I thought that would be enough to keep the sharks at bay. High school can be brutal, especially in a boarding school. I did not, however, count on Wade being a bigger douche than he already is." She bit at a cuticle. "His real name is Paul, by the way. He makes everyone call him Wade. It's not even his middle name."

"Yeah, I figured that out after he told me who his parents were. But you knew?" I asked, outraged.

She nodded, unconcerned with my outrage. I wondered

if Paul's parents even knew he went by Wade. They never mentioned it to me when they told me to look him up.

I didn't know what to say to Kenya. Did I thank her? She did save my life. But she'd also threatened it on multiple occasions and caused my eye to twitch uncontrollably every time she was near.

"You're welcome," she said, the dimple appearing again.

"Yeah, thanks." I poured as much sincerity into the remark as I possibly could.

She laughed out loud, then sobered, her brows drawing together in concern. "What did you see?"

I turned away. "What do you mean?"

"This morning. When you rushed off to the bathroom and threw up. You had a vision, right?" When I didn't answer, she continued. "What did you see?"

Before I could brace for impact, the memory of the visions rushed forth. The memory of her death rushed forth. My eyes stung with the emotions it conjured. "Nothing," I said, my voice hoarse. I cleared my throat and started again. "I didn't see anything."

She scooted around until she was facing me. "Do you know that I've dreamed about you since I was a little girl?"

I frowned at her, discomfort prickling over my skin. Not another admirer. Not another starstruck member of the Order convinced I was going to save the world.

"My parents told me about you when I was five. I didn't really understand at the time, but I knew how special you were, even if you didn't. Even if you still don't."

Just as I was about to tell her exactly how wrong she was, I heard my name like a siren in the night.

"Lorraine!"

Crystal shot inside the ambulance like a laser-guided missile and drew me into a hug. I felt like a rag doll being mauled by a mountain lion, but her hug felt good. I laughed when she held the hug an entire minute too long.

She pulled back and gave me a once-over.

"Was that him?" she asked, her eyes wide in disbelief. "Did Wade send you that note?"

"Yes, he did, Crystal, and my name is actually Lorelei."

"Your real name? You're telling me your real name? What about your witness protection?"

"Witness protection?" Kenya asked, this time with a tad more sarcasm.

"No, I'm sorry. I'm not really in the Witness Protection Program."

She gasped as reality—her reality—sank in. "You're under-cover?"

"Well, not really—"

"Yes," Kenya said, patting my back. "She's undercover, and we can't tell anyone, okay?"

She nodded, her eyes glistening at Kenya then, as though seeing her there for the first time. "Are you undercover, too?"

"Yes," she said again, fighting the comeback of the dimple. "My real name is Katniss Everdeen."

She covered her gaping mouth with her hands, let out something that resembled the squeak of a hamster wheel, then said, "This is the coolest day of my life. Oh, except where Wade tried to kill you. That wasn't cool."

"Thanks," I said, fighting my own grin, but I'd lost Crystal. She was looking past the ambulance door.

Kenya and I leaned over to see what she was ogling. A figure walked forward. One with a familiar shape. A familiar gait. My heart stopped beating as I watched my oldest friend on earth walk forward.

He stopped in front of me, his face full of relief and joy. "Do you just start crap wherever you go?"

"Glitch," I whispered before jumping down and almost tackling him to the ground as I rushed into his arms.

He wrapped them around me and laughed. I laughed, too. Kind of. I mostly sobbed like a girl dumped at prom.

Glitch was one of my very best friends from Riley's Switch.

After a long while, the EMT brought out the Jaws of Life and peeled me off Glitch. By then, I'd finally calmed down enough to ask, "What are you doing here?"

"I came for you."

I couldn't have wiped the smile off my face if he'd paid me to. "I'm glad. I'm ready to go home."

Even though Glitch stood only three inches higher than I did, he seemed to tower over me at that moment. His short black hair and coppery Native American skin glistened under the lamps overhead, as did the green in his hazel eyes, a testament to the fact that his mother was about as Irish as one could get. He was such a beautiful mixture of ethnicities. I'd forgotten how striking he was. Or maybe I'd never known. Never paid attention. But I sure did now. He looked like an angel. A really short angel. One that had lost weight since I saw him last. He looked tired no matter how hard he tried to hide it behind that bright smile of his.

"McAlister."

I turned to where Kenya gestured. The Hamptons were pulling up. They looked like their hearts were broken as they spoke to their son before the police led him to a squad car and put him in the backseat. I could see the venom in his features. He was not going easy on them, his animosity evident in every expression, every sharp movement. That was one conversation I was glad to be excluded from.

After a moment, they looked over at me, their faces full of sadness and regret. It wasn't their fault. Kenya was right. Their son was a douche. Sometimes nature overrode nurture like that. They were good parents. I could see it clearly. Kindness radiated out of them.

I could tell they wanted to apologize, but didn't know what to say. I stepped to them and hugged them both, not entirely certain they would want me to. But they hugged me back with a fierce regard. I was surprised. After everything that had happened, they still thought highly of me.

"I can't believe you came all this way," I said to Glitch when I walked back over. "How is everyone? How is Grandma and Granddad? Brooklyn? Cameron?" I lowered my head. "Jared?"

"They didn't send me, if that's what you mean. Your grandparents."

"I don't understand."

"Brooke and I . . . snooped. We went through your grandparents' mail at the store and found an invoice to this school. Once we figured out where they sent you, I got on a plane. Unfortunately, we couldn't afford for both of us to come. We didn't tell Cameron or Jared. Cameron would have been here before we could blink. He still takes his role very seriously. And Jared." He turned away. "I just don't know what he would have done."

"You found an invoice. I thought . . . I thought they got me a scholarship somehow."

"No. They must have hocked the store to send you here. This place is pricey."

Wonderful. They'd lied to me, then. And Granddad was a pastor, for heaven's sake. "So, they didn't tell you where I was?"

I could feel him withdraw. He resented the fact that no one told him, and I could hardly blame him. I would've felt betrayed as well. I would have felt abandoned.

"No. No one told us. Jared ordered us to leave it alone, said you'd come home when the time was right. But Cameron . . ." He bit the side of his mouth before continuing. "Cameron was furious with your grandparents for a long time. He still is, actually. I'm not sure what he would've done if his dad hadn't been there when he found out. I've never seen him so mad."

Cameron was a part of this whole prophecy thing as well, only from a different standpoint. He'd literally been created. Apparently, when the angels in heaven found out the prophet was going to be born, the one slated to stop the war, they sent an angel down to a human woman, Cameron's mother, to create a protector. They had relations, as my grandfather would say, and nine months later, out popped a bouncing baby nephilim. Since Cameron was part angel, he was much stronger and faster than your average human. And he took his role as protector very seriously. So when Jared first came to town to take me, Cameron was all over him. They fought, almost destroying downtown Riley's Switch in the process, and they still felt a niggling of animosity toward each other, though they now had parallel goals.

"I've seen Cameron angry," I said, remembering the first time they fought. I'd been terrified and awed at the same time.

"Not this angry," Glitch said. "Not this enraged. I thought he would tear apart that store looking for you."

And here I thought I couldn't feel any worse than I already did. "So how are they? My grandparents?"

He released the air from his lungs slowly, letting it slip

through his lips at a leisurely pace as though stalling for time. "What have they told you?"

"That everything is peachy."

"Wow. Never took them for liars."

I knew they had been sugarcoating the truth, but I didn't know how much. I almost dreaded finding out. "What do you mean? What's going on?"

Kenya sat back, watching us, summing up Glitch in her special, homicidal way.

"Things are bad, Lor," he said, bowing his head. "Things are way worse."

I straightened in alarm. "Worse how? I left. Things were supposed to get better."

"They didn't. It seems there are lots of ghosts or spirits or whatever wanting to jump ship before the war, before evil is unleashed upon the earth. Jared's words."

I felt Kenya tense beside me even though she still wore her best poker face.

"They're doing what that spirit Noah did, the first kid who came to us. The spirits are searching out Jared. They want off this plane and they can't get to another one, so by forcing Jared's hand, they're basically committing suicide. Jared has his hands full just trying to hold them all back. It's causing all kinds of unrest. Lots of people have left town, including Ashlee and Sydnee. Their father packed them up and high-tailed it outta Dodge."

When I left Riley's Switch, it looked like he and Ashlee would get together. I wanted to ask how that went, but now was certainly not the time. "I'm sorry, Glitch."

"People just don't know what to think. They're panicking."

I squeezed my lids together until the pressure caused stars to appear behind them. "Grandma and Granddad didn't tell me."

"I'm not surprised. They want you as far away from all that as they possibly can get you. Especially now with all the reporters."

"Reporters?"

"Yeah, you know what happens when a haunted town is bombarded with strange occurrences and unexplainable events. They're having a field day. Fox News and CNN even have a news crew there. They're calling it the beginning of the end. We're getting famous, but the town is falling apart. More and more refugees are showing up with possessed family members. The spirits possessing them want off that plane and the only way out is through Jared."

"I can't even imagine it," I said, perplexed.

"And that's not even the worst of it. People from all over the country have come to be *taken* when the time comes, believing the events point to the Rapture."

"But this isn't the Rapture," I said. "This is a travesty brought on by one insane man."

He grinned at me. "Preaching to the choir, babe. It's been the hardest on your grandparents, but they are handling it all amazingly well even though the town has been really hard on them."

I straightened. "What do you mean? Why?"

"They sent you away," he said with a shrug. "Many members of the Order took that hard, like your grandparents betrayed them, sent their only hope away. Your grandparents have been harassed, ostracized, even attacked."

My hands flew over my mouth. "Attacked? How? What happened?"

"Not physically attacked, but verbally. And the store has been vandalized. Their cars have been egged and keyed. Half the members of the Order have left town, and half of those remaining have taken it upon themselves to punish your grandparents. To let them know just how angry they are."

"Oh, my God, that is so unfair, Glitch."

He wrapped an arm around me. "I know. But through it all, they never gave up your location."

"What is this, World War Two? Are they being interrogated by Nazis?"

He thought about it, then shrugged. "That's a pretty fair comparison."

A bone-crushing guilt rushed through me. I tried the number again, to no avail. "Why aren't they answering my calls?" I asked, beginning to panic.

"I'm not sure. Maybe something happened."

"My God, they went through all this because of me?" A sob wrenched out of my throat before I could stop it.

Glitch pulled me tighter. "Not because of you, Lor. For you. There's a difference."

"I have to go back."

"That's not why I came," he rushed to assure me. "We aren't mad. Well, Cameron is, but for his own reasons. Brooke and I just wanted to know you were okay, so we pooled our money and bought me a plane ticket. I won at rock-paper-scissors."

I looked at him knowingly. "You always win at rock-paper-scissors."

A captivating grin spread across his face. "Yeah, but she doesn't know that. Or she's in denial. Not sure which."

I hugged him. "I've missed you so much."

"That happens when girls are ripped out of my life. It's weird." When I did a half-sob, half-giggle thing, he said, "I missed you, too."

"And I have to go back."

"Lor, I just don't think you should. I think your grand-parents were right. You need to stay hidden."

"No, you don't understand." I looked over at Kenya. "You were right. I had a vision. I had dozens of visions." I squeezed Glitch's hand. "Coming here was a mistake. We are all go-ing to die. The world is going to end, Glitch. I've seen it."

"I brought you so much good news, I thought you'd reciprocate."

"I'm sorry, but it's true. I have to go back. I have to put on my big-girl panties and face this."

His gaze slid past me and he sat slightly devastated for several minutes.

Kenya stood and started punching buttons on her phone. "I'm calling my parents again. I'm coming with you."

I jumped up. "No, Kenya, stay here with them. With your family. Your aunt and uncle."

She glared at me. "Why? So I can die with them? So I can spend my last moments on earth huddling in fear and crying with them?"

I pressed my mouth together in sadness. That was exactly how she was going to die. She saw it on my face and lowered her phone. Her eyes watered. After a moment, she lifted her phone to her ear. "Mom, I need three tickets to New Mex-ico. We need to leave tonight."

"Kenya," I said, my voice breaking, "no. You should be with them."

"Why? In case you fail?"

I nodded.

"Hold on, Mom." She took a menacing step toward me. "In case you don't know the prophecy forward and back-wards like I do, you don't." She poked my chest. Kind of hard. "You don't fail, McAlister. You save us. You save us all, and I want to be there when you do it. I want to see it for myself."

Her faith crushed me. She had no idea just how much I was *not* capable of.

"Okay, Mom, yes, three plane tickets to Albuquerque." She leveled a decided expression on me. "I'm going with her. I'm fighting with her." She gave her mother our information so she could purchase the tickets, then hung up the phone. "My parents will pick us up and drive us to the airport in two hours. They want to meet you." She knelt beside me. "You know, a lot of people think we belong to a cult, like we're a bunch of crazy end-timers, but we don't. We're not. We just believe in the power of good over evil."

"You should be with them, Kenya."

"McAlister, if I'm going to die anyway, if we're all going to die, I'll be with them soon enough. But that's just not going to happen. Sorry, Charlie." She winked at me, the gesture causing a fat tear to push past her lashes. She wiped at it, took a deep breath, and said, "Now, let's go pack."

I didn't have the heart to tell her I'd already done so.

EXCESS BAGGAGE

We stood in the student parking lot waiting for Kenya's parents. The low moon had a delicious fog curling around it and I suddenly realized I was going to miss Maine. But even more, I was going to miss Crystal. She stood beside me, wrenching her hands, wondering exactly what was going on. I was fairly certain she figured out the undercover story was a lie. When Glitch started talking about the reporters that had descended upon Riley's Switch like a pack of vultures again and how this one woman got arrested for going undercover in the high school, pretending to be a student just to get the scoop, I decided to tune him out.

Crystal and I hugged good-bye, her round face and freckled nose buried in my jacket, and she said something about tickets and pliers. I had no idea what she said, but I nodded in agreement anyway.

All together, the flights home took over twelve hours including the layovers in New York and Dallas, but that was a lot better than the three days it took me to get to Maine. My grandparents were waiting for us when we landed at nine o'clock in the morning, unkempt and sodden.

We'd taken the escalators down to baggage claim and waited for the conveyor belt to start its rounds when I heard a feminine voice call out to me.

"Lorelei?"

I turned and saw my grandmother running toward me.

"Grandma!" I cried, and took off at a dead run into her arms. She wrapped me tight in her embrace, but I soon felt another crush as Granddad joined us.

My grandparents took over when my parents disappeared. They took on the burden that was me, changed their lives to accommodate raising another child, one they hadn't expected to have to raise. My grandfather, who was my mother's father, even took over for my father in the Order. He became the pastor of the church and taught the members what he knew, even though it wasn't nearly as much as my father. It was his line through which Arabeth's DNA weaved. All male descendants, for over five hundred years, until me. But when he disappeared, my grandparents took up the cause and kept me safe. They studied the prophecies and taught as best they could. I didn't know where I'd be without them.

We hugged a long time. I didn't know how long, but I was home. Their arms were home. I never thought I could miss anyone so much in my life.

When they finally eased their hold, Granddad framed my face with his weathered hands. He looked exhausted. Disheveled. And I quickly realized Grandma looked much the same.

"We sure missed you, Pix," he said, his gray eyes bright above the shadows under them and wet with emotion.

"I missed you, too."

I looked past Granddad to Brooklyn and got excited all over again. Her thick black hair had been pulled back into a ponytail, and her dark irises sparkled with joy. "Brooke!"

She ran forward. "I missed you, too!"

We hugged a solid minute before breaking the hold. Despite her ecstatic exterior, there was a sadness in the depths of her deep brown eyes. A weariness that hadn't been there before. But I knew Brooke. She wouldn't let me talk about it here in front of the others.

"I forgot how short you are," I said, teasing her since we were both the same height, five-foot-nada.

"And I forgot how flat you are."

I tried to look aghast since that was always my tender subject. While Brooke had blossomed into womanhood recently with the cup size to prove it, I had yet to acquire real girl parts. It was sad. "So, how mad at me are you?" I asked her instead.

"Oh, you have no idea." She waved a dismissive hand in the air. "You'll be paying for this for a very long time."

I smiled, a little in love with the feel of her so close. "I never doubted it for a minute."

She wrapped an arm in mine. "You will be my slave girl

and I shall call you—" She looked up in thought. "—Slave Girl."

"That's creative."

"And you shall be made to scrub my floors and give me mani-pedis on a weekly basis."

I crinkled my nose. "Is that negotiable?"

"Slaves cannot negotiate. They can only slave. But before we begin, there are two boys you might want to say hi to."

She gestured to her side, and sure enough, there were two boys there. Not that I hadn't already noticed all the heads turning their way, but still. My gaze landed on Cameron first. He'd cut his signature blond, shoulder-length hair. It was now short and a little spiky as he leaned against a case displaying historical New Mexican artifacts. He looked fantastic. But he'd stuffed his hands into his pockets and was refusing to look at me.

"He's been a tad angry with us," Grandma said. They'd sent me off in the middle of the night without my created protector. It was no wonder said created protector was a bit miffed.

"So I heard." I walked over to him, inching closer warily like one would with a wild animal. "Do you know how long you're going to be mad at me? Because we have to save the world pretty soon."

Still refusing to even spare me a glance with those crystal blue eyes of his, he said, "I'll let you know when I know."

"Fair enough. Until then, can I have a hug? For old times' sake?"

He kicked at the heel of his other foot. "You didn't ask for one before you left. Figure I don't owe you one now."

Before I could argue that point, he turned and walked out of the building.

I looked over my shoulder at Glitch. "You weren't kidding."

He'd grabbed my bags along with his. "He'll come around."

"I hope so." I said it to Glitch, but my gaze had found its way to the other boy who'd joined us. He was as tall as Cameron, only dark. Stunningly sensual like a Brazilian supermodel. But he looked exhausted as well. His hair needed a trim, and his jaw—sculpted and strong—needed a shave.

He stood in his requisite white T-shirt and jeans with his arms crossed over his chest and a grin lifting one corner of his incredible mouth. His coffee-colored eyes shimmered as he looked at me. "He'll come around if he knows what's good for him," he said.

"Yeah?" I asked, stepping toward him. I didn't want to get too gooey in front of my grandparents, but this was Jared Kovach. The love of my life. And the Angel of Death, but still.

"You going to offer me one of those?" he asked.

"What? A hug?"

He reached out and ran the backs of his fingers over my hand. His touch was like electricity. It sent a jolt of pleasure rocketing through me, weakened my knees, accelerated my heart. Without any further ado, I jumped into his arms. He caught me like I knew he would—because he was super strong and could do things like that—and held me tight.

"I'm so sorry," I said.

"Lorelei, you don't ever have to apologize to me."

"But I just left and I've made things worse."

Still holding me a foot off the ground, he leaned back and questioned me with a gaze. Granddad had his hand on Jared's back in a gesture of affirmation, while Grandma smiled over Jared's shoulder at me.

"Something happened," I said, hating to break the news

so soon after our long-awaited greeting, but they needed to know. "Something changed."

Granddad nodded. "What do you say we get to the car and talk there?"

"Okay. Oh, I almost forgot!" Jared let me slide down his body to the ground and I savored the feel of him before turning to our newest team member. "This is Kenya."

She stepped forward, her usual brusque confidence all but gone. She nodded a greeting.

"We know who you are, honey," Grandma said. "Your mother called, told us you'd be joining us. We're thrilled to have such an adventurer on our side."

As they shook hands, I asked, "Adventurer? What do you mean, adventurer?"

Granddad chuckled and shook her hand as well. "She didn't tell you?" he asked.

"No." I glared at her accusingly. We'd just spent twelve hours on airplanes and in airports. She could have mentioned something about being an adventurer. Not that I had any idea what that meant exactly.

"I'm so honored to meet you," she said to him. But when Jared held out his hand for his turn, her expression changed from reverence to doubt. If I didn't know any better, I'd say she was afraid of him. To her credit, she held her ground and took his hand into hers. Her voice dropped to a husky whisper. "Your Grace," she said, clearly knowing who, and what, Jared was.

Because Jared was an archangel, a prince of heaven, many of our members insisted on addressing him as "Your Grace." It wasn't something he encouraged, but nobody listened when he discouraged it, so he just went along with the majority.

"Kenya. Nice to meet you."

She pulled away as quickly as she could without being blatantly rude and cleared her throat.

"Don't worry," Jared said, leaning in to her. "If I were here for you, I wouldn't shake your hand first."

Sadly, we all burst out laughing, the tension was so taut, and I was worried poor Kenya would faint dead away. She did turn a lovely shade of green when he mentioned his job. So that was nice.

My grandparents had brought the church van, so we all fit quite nicely. We sat in the airport parking lot. Jared sat beside me in the middle seat. He held my hand, seeming to know I'd need the support as I explained what had happened.

"I was bombarded with visions yesterday. Everything changed. One minute I'm having visions about a fender bender here or a broken nail there, and the next—" I swallowed hard and Jared squeezed. "—the next, I'm seeing the end of the world."

Granddad lowered his head in thought as Grandma shot him a worried look.

"It's going to be like a storm. Like when Mom and Dad disappeared," I said to them. "Low thunder clouds. A deafening wind. Rain. And darkness. A darkness that seems endless, like a fog or smoke that has the will to go where it wants. To do what it wants."

"Demons?" Glitch asked.

"I think some are demons and some are spirits like we saw before. They will take over the earth. They'll kill everyone. Everywhere. My leaving did nothing. It didn't help at all."

"Pix, your leaving accomplished what we wanted it to. It kept you safe until it was time for you to come home."

"You knew? You knew I would have to come home?"

"Of course they did," Kenya said. "You can't outrun destiny."

"She has a point," Brooke tossed in. She was so helpful.

"I thought my leaving might change things. Might make things better."

"It did," Grandma said. "It kept you safe. Out of harm's way."

"But not for you," I said to her. "Glitch told me what you've been going through. I'm so sorry."

Grandma reached over and took my free hand. "Don't you dare apologize. We knew exactly what we were getting into. We knew some would be very angry." When she leveled an accusing stare on Cameron, he simply turned and did his signature distant stare out the window.

It would have been funny if not for the fact that it was all so serious. So blindingly real.

"You could have been hurt," I said to them.

"Pixie Stick," Granddad said, his voice stern, "stop worrying about us this minute. We did what was best at the time. If some don't agree, it's because they don't love you like we do."

"I love her," Cameron shot out, completely offended. "You sent her off without me. Me! Her protector. I should have been with her."

"That's why we had Kenya," Grandma said.

The fact that my grandparents knew about Kenya shouldn't have surprised me, but it did.

Cameron looked at her anew, his astonishment palpable. "Her? This walking bleach factory? She's human."

Well, that answered that. I was beginning to wonder.

"And," Kenya said, raising her chin a notch, "I'm a third-degree black belt in tae kwon do, an expert markswoman, and I'm certified to carry a concealed weapon in seven states, including this one. My parents have been training me since I was a toddler. So bite my ass."

Brooke and I gasped at her use of the word "ass" in front of my grandparents, his being a minister and all, but they hid grins.

Cameron leaned over to her. "You're still just a human."

"And I saved your charge's ass from a psychotic douche."

Yep, we gasped again. If she did that any more, we'd probably hyperventilate.

"Where were you?" she continued.

When Cameron leaned even closer to her, Glitch leaned in between them. "We get it, Cameron," he said. "You're mad. Now, leave her alone. She did your job for you. The least you can do is say thank you."

Cameron bit down, worked his jaw, then gathered his resolve and grinned at him. But it was his evil grin, the one he saved for special occasions and for tormenting Glitch, his favorite pastime.

"Can we get back to the 'end of the world' thing?" Brooke asked. "It seems kind of important."

She took Cameron's face between her hands and forced him to focus on her until his anger melted. Without taking his eyes off Brooke, he said, "Fine, then. Thank you."

His expression of gratitude surprised everyone, but what surprised me was the look of forlornness on Kenya's face when she glanced at Glitch. Glitch! She had a thing for him. For Glitch! I sat speechless and wondered if Glitch was still seeing Ashlee. There could be another war on the horizon if so. Messing with the Southern Belles was never a good idea, third-degree black belt or not.

"Maybe you could take another look," Kenya said,

recovering. She cast a pointed stare at me. "Maybe things have changed. We took care of the threat at Bedford Fields, the catalyst for your new visions. Maybe we set things right again."

The only reason I wasn't seeing the deaths of everyone I was hugging was because I was using every ounce of mental energy I could spare to block my visions. I didn't want to see the deaths of my grandparents. My best friends. Jared. Would Jared die in all this? Could he? I had no idea, but I sure didn't want to find out.

"Here," Kenya said. She held out her hand to me, encouraging me to take another look, to see if her future was still dire, full of fear and death.

I winced and scooted out of her reach. I'd already looked when she was sleeping at JFK. I just barely touched her, barely opened my mind to a vision, and I instantly felt fear rip at my chest so hard and so fast, I snatched my hand back like I'd been burned. I wasn't about to repeat the experience.

"We didn't set things right. I've already looked. Nothing has changed." I crossed my arms over my chest. "We need to find out who opens those gates. Who opened them in the first place when I was six. We need to know for sure if it's the same person. Did you find anything on a Dyson?" I asked my grandparents.

A group of nephilim had come for me before. They were watered-down versions of Cameron. Even with centuries of breeding with pure humans, siphoning the celestial DNA out of them, they were strong. Much stronger than normal humans. We defeated them, but the leader told me who sent them. A man named Dyson.

"That's who we need to be looking for. If we can just

stop him from opening the gates again, won't this all be over?"

"In theory," Granddad said. "Villanueva is looking into it, but there are a lot of Dysons out there." Villanueva was our sheriff and a member of the Order. Having the county sheriff on our side came in really handy, especially when it came time to explain certain unexplainable events.

I nodded. "At least we're looking in the right direction." Or I hoped we were. "I've tried to remember more about him. Anything. But my memory of that day just isn't that great. I've even tried to draw him."

I pulled out my sketchpad and showed them what I remembered. I'd done a rough drawing of the man, his short blond hair whipping about his head, his light blue shirt stained with his own blood because the best image I had of him in my mind was when I—no, we, Malak-Tuke and I together—had stabbed him with a stick. Leaves flew about us as he scrambled back, his eyes wide in astonishment. He'd summoned Malak-Tuke for himself. He'd wanted to be possessed by him, to control him, but apparently Satan's second-in-command had other ideas. When he'd entered me, when I'd swallowed him whole, breathed him in, the man went wild with anger.

I closed the sketchbook when I realized it was doing no one any good. I doubted if they knew him that they'd recognize him from my six-year-old's memory and amateurish drawing. "We have to keep looking. It seems our only shot at stopping this war before it starts is finding this man's identity."

"And stopping him," Glitch said.

Granddad started the van and we headed back to Riley's Switch. It would take a little over an hour to get there, which meant I had a little over an hour to snuggle with Jared. I leaned back against him and squirmed until I found just the right spot. He laughed softly and nipped at my ear.

"You have to tell me everything," Brooklyn said from over the back of my seat.

I couldn't help but notice how much effort she put into avoiding eye contact with Cameron. Surely they'd kiss and make up eventually.

"I want to know all about Maine. And the kids there. And boarding schools. They seem so foreign."

"They are," I said with a grin. "They definitely take some getting used to."

"A little different from Riley High?" she asked, one corner of her mouth rising.

"A lot different." Then I thought about it. After a quick glance toward Kenya, I said, "And yet not so much."

Brooke nodded in understanding. "Did you keep up with your exercises?"

I rolled my eyes. "Yes, Mom." She was always pushing me to try to see more. In my visions. In pictures. I remembered one such exercise and grabbed my bag to rake through it. Finding the picture I had of us in the fifth grade, I took it out and showed it to her accusingly. "You took Mrs. Bradshaw's paperweight."

"What?"

"You took it. The whole class got in trouble, and you're the one who took it."

She snorted, indignant. "I so did not."

I narrowed my eyes on her. "I was there," I said, shaking the evidence at her. "I saw the whole thing. She made you mad when she wouldn't let you go to the bathroom because you'd just been, so you took her dragon paperweight when she was busy snapping pictures."

After several false starts at a comeback, she switched directions. "I put it back the next day," she said, more than a little disconcerted. "Maybe you don't need to practice quite that much. Don't want to overdo, you know? Pull a brain muscle or something." She tapped her head for emphasis.

"Yeah, that's what I thought." I gave her my best tough girl attitude, channeling Kenya.

Unfortunately, Kenya picked up on it and leveled a deadpan expression on me.

"What?" Brooke and I said in unison.

BETTY AND THE BARCALOUNGER

Driving through Riley's Switch after so long an absence caused a lump to form in my throat. The warmth of nostalgia spread through me as we passed familiar trees, schools, and the small businesses that lined Main Street. But all that stopped when we hit the square. Glitch was right. We'd been invaded by the media.

News vans littered the area around the courthouse and gravitated toward the Traveler's Inn, one of our more famous structures. People swore it was haunted and we'd had everything from ghost hunters to novelists visit to get a glimpse of the lady in white. But the news vans and all the visitors were like blemishes on our small town. I realized how selfish I was being. The world would want to know about all the strange activities going on, but having the signs of the apocalypse, the one that I was supposed to stop, advertised all over the world upped the stress levels already coursing through my veins.

And then I saw them. Sprinkled among the throngs of sightseers snapping pictures and end-timers praying en masse were those who were just a little bit different. They stood in the middle of all the chaos and yet apart, their stares vacant as we passed by. A blond woman in her thirties. An elderly man with a gray beard. A young girl no older than myself with dark circles under her red-rimmed eyes and a snarl on her mouth. They watched us as we slid past. No, they watched Jared. These were the possessed people Glitch told us about.

I turned an astonished gaze on him, but he was busy staring back through glittering, dark eyes, as though promising their fates would end soon.

Then we pulled up to my grandparents' store. My home. We lived in the back of the store and my bedroom was upstairs, above it. I never thought I'd be so happy to see that old store, but I was a little shocked at the state in which I found it. Most of the plate glass windows were broken and either had to be boarded up or duct-taped. One corner had been spray-painted, but not tagged as one would expect. It was a threat. An accusation. All it said was TRAITOR.

I looked away from the evidence of what my grandparents had been going through on my behalf, and anger coursed through me. How dare they treat my grandparents with such disrespect after everything they'd done for the church, for the town. A thought—so small, it barely took root before I pushed it away—flashed in my mind. Why would I want to save people like that? Why would I want to risk my life to help those who treated my grandparents so horribly?

But I couldn't think like that. The mere idea caused a wave of nausea. How dare *I* judge them. That made me no better than those who would behave so callously.

Several old friends and members of the congregation were waiting for us at home. They'd organized a potluck, and Betty Jo, my grandma's best friend, was busy setting out utensils when we walked in through the store. She stopped, her round face full of relief and joy and something that resembled hope. I tried not to let it weigh me down. She was a member of the Order. She knew what was supposed to happen just like the rest of us. She knew the premonitions where I was concerned. And she believed.

I set my jaw. Tried to believe with her as she rushed forward and wrapped me into her soft arms. Getting hugged by Betty Jo was like getting hugged by an overstuffed Barcalounger, comforting and warm.

"We have missed the dickens out of you," she said when she set me at arm's length. "Your grandmother has been beside herself."

"Now, now, Betty Jo," Grandma chided, a soft warning in her tone that only someone who knew her as well as Betty Jo and I would pick up on. "I have been just fine."

A look that I could only describe as horror flashed across Betty's face, and I almost laughed out loud. Clearly Grandma was a big fat liar. I'd have to tease her about that later.

"Right," Betty said. "Fine." She winked at me and I smothered a giggle.

Sheriff Villanueva came in through the store then, his

arms full with ice in one hand and a casserole dish in the other. "Mrs. Chavez said this needs to go in the oven." He stopped then and, after looking me up and down, dropped his load on the breakfast bar and came forward for a hug, too. I'd never hugged the sheriff before, but he was part of our family if anyone was. He'd been there for us when we needed him most.

"Good to see you, kid."

I offered him my very best grateful smile. "Thank you for sticking by them."

He shrugged it off. "Wouldn't dream otherwise."

We followed the hum of voices. A few of our closest friends were grilling hamburgers and talking about the strangest things they'd seen so far, each trying to one-up the other.

Many of our congregation were there, people rushing around preparing for a cookout. Most came up and hugged me. It was a nice homecoming. But a few didn't. They were clearly just as angry with me as they were with my grandparents, and that made me angry. I wanted to rail at them. Turn on my cyclone-with-arms trick. But that hadn't worked very well the first time. I could take only so much humiliation.

Kenya fixed herself a plate after some preemptive introductions and said to me, "Seems like a lot of your grandfather's parishioners are a little peeved with him."

The feelings of resentment came crashing through again. "How dare they try to dictate what we do. It's our lives. My life."

She shrugged and crunched a chip. "You can't be too mad at them."

Brooklyn's jaw came unhinged. "Yes, we can. They don't have the right to try to tell Lor or her grandparents what to do. How to live their lives."

"You have to understand," Kenya said, "they believe in you. They believe you are going to save them from whatever is coming. When you left, they felt abandoned. You need to try to see it from their side."

"Well, their side is stupid," Brooke said, stealing a chip off Kenya's plate. "They don't know what Lorelei has been through."

Kenya eyed Brooke as though she was going to shank her for grand larceny. It was a tense moment. After coming to her senses, she said, "True heroes are never heroes for the recognition. They do what they are supposed to do, play the hand they've been dealt."

"Is that what you think?" I asked, my mouth hanging open. It couldn't have been appealing. "That I want recognition? I never asked for this. I never wanted to be this great prophet who is supposed to figure out how to stop this stupid war. I don't expect anything, especially a pat on the back."

The barest hint of a smile tilted her mouth. "And true heroes don't seek out their heroism. It's thrust upon them. Kind of like what's happening to you." She winked at me and strode away as Brooke and I both just stood there like bumps on a log.

"She sucks," Brooke said, indignant. "She's way too calm about this whole thing. Too logical."

"Right? Since when does logic enter into anything we do?"

"Exactly."

Dinner was wonderful. We had a kitchen full of food, including my grandmother's famous green chile stew, Betty Jo's amazing asparagus casserole, and Mrs. Chavez's hand-rolled tamales. I ate more in that one meal than I did the entire time I was in Maine. Unless one were to count seafood. I pretty much ate my weight in seafood.

Brooke and Glitch wanted to know everything. I told them what I could about Maine as we sat in plastic chairs, drinking orange soda around a fire pit. I explained how we only *assumed* we had the whole layering thing down. "They have that stuff down in Maine. It's layer up or die a slow and painful death."

They nodded in understanding. But could they ever truly understand the depths of my near-hypothermic experience?

Still, Maine was kind of cool. I'd certainly miss Crystal.

With the sun dipping low on the horizon, I strolled as nonchalantly as I could over to Cameron. He'd eaten and was busy surveying the surroundings. He had yet to say ten words to me.

"Hey," I said, taking a sip of orange soda and leaning against the building beside him.

He offered me a quick glance, then went back to scowling at the dirt. The dirt probably deserved it.

"I love your hair. It really suits your face." And it did. He was a handsome guy, even when glowering like now.

But I got nothing. Not even a nod of acknowledgment.

"I'm sorry. If that helps." When he still didn't reply, I continued. "I thought maybe if I left, things would change. They'd stop. Maybe this war wouldn't happen."

"Do you think I give a damn about this stupid war?" he asked as though appalled. "I'm not here to fight a war, Lorelei. I'm here to keep you alive. Remember? That's why I was created in the first place. I should have gone with you."

I blinked in surprise. "If I'd made you go with me, what do you think that would have done to Brooke? Your girlfriend is my best friend. You forget that sometimes."

"She's not my girlfriend."

I'd noticed a strained silence between them all the way back. Brooke could hide things well, but clearly something was wrong.

"What happened?" I asked him; then I glared at him and rephrased my question. "What did you do?"

He straightened. "Me? I didn't do anything. She's the one full of piss and vinegar."

I kind of gaped at him. First, I'd only ever heard my grandparents use the piss-and-vinegar phrase. And second . . . "Brooke is mad at you? Why?"

"She says I have no right to be angry. With you." He said the last bit accusingly, then leaned closer. "But I do have that right."

Uh-oh. My running off in the middle of the night had caused more damage than I thought it would.

"She'll get over it," I said. "I'm sorry. I didn't mean to cause a rift between you two."

Maybe that was the root of his anger.

"I'm not worried about Brooklyn's temper either, Lor. I thought . . . I was created for one purpose only. My entire existence is because of you. If I can't protect you, what good am I? What is my purpose?"

"Is that what you think? That your only worth lies in protecting me?"

He snorted. "Duh."

I almost laughed. I'd never heard him use the word "duh" before, either. If "duh" could be considered a word. "Did you ever think that maybe this whole thing is because of me? Maybe if I'd never been born, it would never have begun?"

"That's not egocentric at all."

He had a point. "Okay, sorry. But don't you think it's possible? I mean all the prophecies say that the last prophet of

Arabeth will stop the war before it even begins. Maybe my birth was some kind of catalyst to the end of times."

His hard gaze turned almost sympathetic, but not in a nice, caring way. "The only thing your birth catalyzed was the constant pain in my ass."

Well, that was uncalled for. But again, he had a point.

Jared's gaze followed me as I said my hellos to our friends. Mr. Moore only glared at me when I greeted him, but he was relieved to have me back. I could tell. Mrs. Henderson and the Dixon sisters were almost giddy to have me back. It was sweet. And there were new members, too. I knew their faces, but they'd never been members of our church, much less members of the Order.

"Granddad, is everyone here members of our super-secret club?"

"Sure are." When he noticed where my gaze landed, he added, "We've had a few people come to us looking for answers. The whole town has been dealt a tricky hand." He glanced down at me, his eyes sad. "I guess it's time to set things right."

"I don't suppose you've figured out how I'm supposed to do that?"

He bit down, gestured toward Grandma and the rest of the gang, and took my hand. "I need to show you something."

Granddad gave the cue to the rest of the Scooby gang and herded us down our creepy stairs that led to our even creepier basement. It was not my favorite place to be, and yet it still held memories. Creepy memories, but memories just the same. Being in the shadowy room flooded me with feelings of nostalgia. It surprised me and I took a moment to absorb those feelings, pretending I was allowing my eyes to adjust to the darkness. I'd never been so glad to be in a creepy place.

A single bulb burned overhead as Granddad took down an old box off a shelf. It was my father's stuff. I'd riffled through it before. It was how I found out that my paternal grandfather was not only still alive, but he lived close by, doing fifteen to twenty in the state pen.

Granddad gestured for me to sit on an old sofa we should have thrown out years ago. He sat the box on a rickety table my grandmother had refused to get rid of because I'd made it in middle school. It was a constant reminder of one field I should never go into: woodworking.

Brooke and Glitch took up half the sofa, too. They scrunched together so Grandma could sit beside me, while Jared stood against the arm, close enough to touch my shoulder. Kenya seemed to feel like a fifth wheel. She scanned the small room, trying to figure out where to stand. She chose to sit on the other arm of the sofa, the one by Glitch. He smiled up at her when she did so. Oh, yeah. There was definitely something there.

Cameron was busy being Cameron. He stayed near the stairs. Still refusing to join in the fun. Pouter. I wanted to tell him his face was going to freeze like that, but he probably wasn't as gullible as I was. In my own defense, I was seven the last time I fell for the frozen-face thing. Possibly eight.

"I've scoured the ancient texts for years," Granddad said. "Studied the prophecies that talked about the end of times. But there were several things I never noticed until recently." He raked through the contents of the box, looking for something specific. He paused to focus his attention. "For one, there is one text that talks about you going into hiding before the war. It's short and easy to miss."

My ears perked up. "You mean like I did?" I asked, astonished.

He nodded. "They speak of you going into hiding in a place that is void of the sun."

"Granddad," I said, grinning, "Maine has sunlight. Just not as much as we do."

"Exactly," he said, slapping a hand on the table. "That is exactly what I want you to realize. To know deep in your heart, Pix. These texts are translated from the original documents. Some of them were in French. Some in Italian. But all those from Arabeth were in a very old form of Gaelic. They had to be translated, and because of that, they were diluted. The original meanings, the truest sources, are lost." He fixed a pointed stare on me, willing me to understand his deeper message. "What I'm trying to get across to you, to all of you, is that we have to take everything the documents say with a grain of salt."

"So, you're saying don't take them literally?" Brooke asked.

"Kind of. I mean, there are just some aspects that are going to be inaccurate."

Hope spread through me like a warm blush. "You mean, they could be wrong? I may not be the prophet? This whole war thing may not hinge on me?"

He dropped his gaze. "No. I'm sorry, hon. That part is pretty clear."

"But you just said—"

"Pix." He pressed his mouth together, searching for the right words. After a moment, he said, "There are too many prophecies, too many accounts, to dispute that part. Too many predictions from your other ancestors, from the other prophets up the line. What I'm saying now is, a lot was left out."

"Like what?" I asked, trying to squelch the disappointment sinking into me.

Grandma put her hand on my arm. "We have been scouring the archives since you left. Looking for clues. On how to stop this. On how to help you. On how it all ends."

"And?" I asked with more hope than I'd wanted to.

"We can't find anything that explains how you do it. They only say that you do. Over and over and over. You just do." She patted my knee. "In all fairness, Pix, the prophets before you may not have been *able* to see how you do it."

Granddad bent his head.

"There's more," I said to him. "I can tell."

He kneeled beside me, put his hand over Grandma's. "It's just that, there's something else we never realized until recently. It never occurred to us."

"Okay."

"All the prophecies, every single one of them, talk about events through history, give accounts of things that came to pass decades, even centuries ago. They all lead up to the present time, but they end at the same time. They talk about the dark days leading up to the war, the trials and tribulations you overcome, your going into hiding, the dissention in the church when you do so, and then it just says you come back to where it all started and you stop the war before it ever begins. In the blink of an eye, it just stops."

"I don't understand. Everything just stops?"

"Everything. There isn't another word anywhere about what happens after. It's as though—"

"As though they couldn't see any further," I said, filling in the pieces. A soft shock wave rippled through me. "Like the world ends and there's nothing left to see." I looked up at him.

"Sweetheart, they all say the same thing. They all say you'll stop this."

"Granddad," I began, but stopped before my voice broke, trying for once in my miserable life to quell my fear, to hold it at bay and not start crying like a schoolgirl who spilled her Kool-Aid on her new dress. I felt Jared's reassuring caress at my shoulder. "Granddad, you don't understand. I saw how the world ends." I scrubbed my face with my fingers before continuing. "I don't stop anything. My own visions have proved that."

Every time I thought of all those visions, of all those deaths, I started down the dark and lonely path known as hyperventilation. Panic tightened my chest.

Grandma took my hand to draw me back to her. "Pix, you were destined to stop this the moment you were born." Her eyes shimmered with emotion in the low light. "You will succeed. We know it. We just . . . we don't know how. And we don't know what comes next." When she looked up at Cameron, her eyes were filled with tears. I was clearly missing something.

"What are you trying to say, exactly? What could be worse than all this?"

Cameron stuffed his hands into his jeans pockets and kicked the floor at his feet before speaking. "They're saying there's no more. It all ends."

"Yes," I said, growing annoyed. "I got that part."

Jared spoke then. "They're saying, there are no more prophecies. And since you are the last prophet, they're saying they don't know if you survive."

Their meaning dawned and I nodded slowly. "So, you're worried I'll die trying to stop this war."

Grandma bowed her head. "We just— We're not sure

how to take the fact that there are no more visions. How to interpret it."

"A grain of salt," Granddad said. Still kneeling before me, he rubbed my knee reassuringly. "We have to take everything with a grain of salt."

I could try to do that. I really liked salt.

"After all of our searching in the archives, we found something in your father's belongings."

They pulled out an old journal. I'd been through the box before and didn't notice it, but at the time I'd been looking for official documents like birth and death certificates, anything on my paternal grandfather.

"Was it Dad's?" I asked.

They glanced at each other uncertainly.

"We aren't sure how your father came across this book," Granddad said, "but he had it among some other things that belonged to your grandpa Mac. And Sheriff Villanueva confirmed that there's blood on it."

"Blood?" I asked as I took it from them, noting the brown stains that must have been the dark red color of blood at one time. My fingers tingled when they touched the leather cover, and a wave of electricity started at the tips and traveled up my hands. It was not a comfortable feeling. Brooke leaned over for a better view.

Before I could ask any more questions, someone called out from overhead. "Is anyone down there?"

We turned to a deep male voice and watched as a man descended the stairs, his heavy footsteps against the wooden slats causing dust to puff around him and fall over the sides.

"We're here," Granddad said, his brows drawn in curiosity.

"They told me where to find you." The man ducked past

the cement ceiling, a huge smile on his face. "I've come to join the fight. Where do I sign up?"

"Mac?" I asked, my voice soft with astonishment. "Grandpa Mac?"

He stepped off the last stair and waited, let me absorb the impossibility of his presence. We all stood. My grandparents seemed just as astonished as I was.

"What are you—? How did you get out?"

The last time I'd left Mac, he was sitting on the other side of a glass partition and we were speaking to each other through the intercom system at the Central New Mexico Correctional Facility in Los Lunas. We'd pressed our hands to the glass and he let me see what happened to him. To his wife, too. My paternal grandmother. She'd died the day I was born, protecting me. And he went after the men who tortured and killed her, took every single one of them out before finding her lifeless body tied to a chair. Though he was only trying to get his wife back, he'd taken the law into his own hands and killed people in the process. But the prison sentence he received because of it did nothing to evoke remorse. He would've done it again if he could have, would have killed them all again, he hated the monsters that much. But he did it out of love. An extreme devotion to the woman who stole his heart at a sock hop in '53. They'd taken her from him, and that was not an easy thing to forget.

His teeth flashed a movie star smile. "I broke out," he said, pleased with himself. "Told you, I came to join the fight." Mac was tall but thick, his build solid. He had graying red hair with about a week's worth of scruff on his chin. It made him look rugged and kind at the same time, but that smile was straight from Hollywood.

My utter amazement, my absolute astonishment took a

backseat to the relief that flooded my entire body. I didn't know why, but his presence was as welcome as rain after a seven-year drought. As a direct descendant of Arabeth, he knew things that my maternal grandparents didn't. He'd grown up with the prophecies, had studied them from the time he was a child. He even had a touch of the gift himself, though supposedly the visions were passed on only to the females in the line.

I stepped to him, trying to contain my glee. "It's good to see you."

"It's good to see you, too," he said. His face resembled my father's—the red hair, the soft gray eyes, the scruffy jaw—so much so, I wanted to touch it, to run my hands over his stubble.

Without waiting another moment, he pulled me into his arms and hugged me to him.

"Mac," my grandfather—my other grandfather—said at my back. I looked over my shoulder as Mac shook hands with him first then my grandmother while keeping me locked in his embrace. "It's been a long time."

"Yes, it has," Mac said. "I wanted to thank you for all you've done." He gave me a hard squeeze and kissed the top of my head.

"It was our pleasure," Granddad said. "I can assure you."

"And these are my friends," I said, a tad ecstatic. I took turns introducing them, not quite sure how to introduce Kenya, but when I got to Jared, Mac's expressions change. Jared's did, too. A knowing air came over their faces. A recognition.

Jared held out his hand, but Mac stepped back a little and gave him a once-over, offering him the most devilish grin I'd ever seen. Then he took Jared's hand in a firm shake, as though thanking him. As though grateful.

"We've met," he said to me.

"Yes, sir," Jared said, matching Mac's attitude, devilish grin for devilish grin. "We have."

"I owe you for this," Mac said, indicating his surroundings.

"It's a present." Jared gestured toward me. "For that one."

"What do you mean?" I asked them, burning to be let in on the secret.

But apparently Cameron knew more than the rest of us. "That's what you were up to last night," he said to Jared, his lids narrowing. "You broke him out of prison."

Several soft gasps echoed in the room as Mac's expression confirmed Cameron's suspicions.

"He sure did," Mac said.

Jared lifted one shoulder, dismissing the whole thing. "I just set into motion a series of events that would give someone who was, say, very alert the means to slip by a few guards unnoticed."

"You really escaped from prison?" Brooke asked.

"Yes, ma'am, I did," he said to her, "with a little help." Then he planted a resentful gaze on Jared. "But really? The garbage collections? You couldn't come up with a better escape route?"

Jared quirked one brow. "Seemed like a good idea at the time."

"Now that you're here," Granddad said to Mac, "can you tell us anything about this journal?"

Mac's smile faded when he spotted it. "Lucas found it."

Lucas, my dad. "Was it yours?" I asked. "There's blood on it."

We'd stunned him. He didn't respond for a long while, then he said, "That would be your grandmother's blood."

Every muscle in my body grew rigid.

"I found it stuffed into the waistband of her pants when I found her." His eyes watered with the memory. "I had no idea whose it was. I figured she'd found it and hid it from the men who took her, so I put it in the floorboards of the house after the shoot-out that night before the cops got there. I didn't think I was going to survive. I didn't want to survive." It took him a moment to gather himself. I laced my fingers into his and he looked down at me with a love I was certain I didn't deserve. My grandmother had died protecting me. How could he get past that? How could he love me still? "When I was recovering in the hospital," he continued, "handcuffed to the bed, I told your dad where to find it. I was never certain if he did or not."

"What is it?" Brooke asked, angling for a better view.

"Sadly, I had no idea why Olivia stashed it. It's just a bunch of drawings. Nothing important that I could tell. But you," he said, setting me at arm's length, his expression stern. "You can figure it out, I'm certain."

I shook my head, but he took my chin into a soft grip.

"Do you think I escaped prison to watch the world end, Lorelei?" When I shrugged, he said, "I'm here to watch you succeed, Pix. I can feel the doubt inside you, but there is none inside me. Not an inkling."

I wanted to list all the ways I was going to fail him, to fail them all, but now was not the time and we were interrupted anyway.

"We're going to head out," a man said through the basement opening. Mr. Gibson, an elder member of our church, took a few steps down and poked his head through the opening. "Glad to have you back, Lorelei."

"Thanks, Mr. G."

Granddad called up to him, "Don't key my truck again."

"Bill," he said, seeming exasperated. "I only keyed Vera's car. I had nothing to do with that picture of Satan on your fender."

They were clearly kidding, but it caused a quake of regret inside me. Granddad sensed it and put an arm around me to pull me closer.

"Don't you dare, Pix," he said softly at my ear. "Doing the right thing is not always the easy thing."

I nodded, pretending to brush it off, pretending to agree.

Exhaustion set in soon after people started leaving. Betty Jo wrapped me in her bearlike embrace before heading out. I didn't want Brooke or Glitch to leave, but they seemed dead set on doing that very thing. We all promised to see each other at school the next day, because in my grandparents' excitement, they reenrolled me. I tried to look excited when they told me, but when they laughed softly to themselves, I realized how badly I'd failed. And even though they said I didn't have to go since the world was about to end and all, I decided I wanted to go. I wanted my old life back, even if it was only for a few hours.

Normally at such a time, everyone would be staying the night. Brooke had her own bed in my room and Glitch always slept on the floor with a sleeping bag. Before I'd left for Maine, even Cameron would stay over, keeping watch from my window seat. Jared was now living in the apartment behind our store. His closeness made me feel safe and a little giddy.

But I had Kenya to think about now. She could take the extra bed in my room. Cameron disappeared without saying a word and Jared kissed my cheek congenially before going to his apartment behind the store.

I got the feeling my grandparents wanted to talk to Mac alone. Grandma made coffee as I gave my two grandfathers a quick kiss on the cheek before they headed into our living room.

"I want you to get some rest," Grandma said as I gave her a kiss, too.

"I can't make any promises, Grandma. My new roommate is a party animal."

Kenya's expression deadpanned as she followed me up the narrow stairs.

"I mean it!" Grandma called out to us.

"Me, too!" I called back. "If you hear dancing and a live band, just ignore it."

I had yet to reacquaint myself with my room. It was just as I'd left it, only cleaner. My peach-colored bedspread lay rumple-free atop its twin bed, the one that used to house a canopy when I was a kid. The other twin bed, the one my grandparents bought for Brooklyn, sat against the far wall, its thick comforter also crisp and rumple-free. My computer sat on the white desk Granddad had put together for me when I was in middle school. Everything in its place. Walking into my room was different. Warmer. More welcoming than even my grandma's kitchen.

I missed my friends already, so imagine my thrill when they showed up on my fire escape. I startled when a smiling face appeared out of the darkness. Then another. Glitch put a finger over his lips to shush me while Brooke gestured me forward.

I unlocked the giant window and Brooke and Glitch crawled inside. Holy cow, I loved having my own escape route.

Jared stood behind them. "Got room for one more?"

Narrowing my eyes on him, I said, "I thought that good-bye felt a little fake."

He grinned and ducked inside. Even Cameron came in, cranky disposition and all.

My gang was back together. Life was good.

"We need a plan," Brooke said, doing a 180 into Serious-ville. "If the world is ending in three days, we'd best be fig-uring out how to stop it."

I had to agree with her. "If you have any new light to shed on the subject, I'm all ears."

"We have to figure out who this Dyson guy is," Kenya said, clearly on top of it. "What do we know about him?"

Unfortunately, not a lot. Dyson was the only name we had to go on, the one the descendants of nephilim gave us when they'd come after me. They said Dyson had sent them, but they also indicated that he was the man who opened the gates in the first place.

It was so weird to think of Kenya as being on my side after all the crap she put me through. I still wasn't quite over it. "You could have clued me in," I said to her, my every word dripping with resentment, "when you pulled the switchblade on me."

Brooklyn gasped. "You pulled a switchblade on her?"

A mirthful smirk flashed across Kenya's face. "Like you've never thought about it."

"Good point."

I played along and looked at Brooke in astonishment. "You've thought about pulling a switchblade on me? What kind of a best friend would do that?"

"Not so much a switchblade," she said, her forehead crin-kling in thought. "But there was a paring knife close by one time when we were arguing. Illicit thoughts danced across my brain."

"Brooke!"

"Only for a second," she said in her own defense. "And they didn't involve me actually stabbing you. It was more of a love poke."

"Oh."

"Hardly any blood."

I hid a grin. "Okay, then."

"So, this guy?" Kenya said, picking up where she left off. "The one who's supposed to open the gates? What do we know about him?"

I riffled through my backpack and brought out the drawing once again. "This is pretty much it," I said, handing it over.

She studied it. "Those nephilim that came for you, they said his name was Dyson?"

"Yes."

We weren't getting anywhere very fast. Keyna could study my drawing all day, and the only thing she'd come away with was eyestrain. I took it back from her. She glared.

Brooklyn scooted closer to me. "Are you thinking what I'm thinking?"

"Unless you're thinking that we're all going to die screaming, then probably not."

She patted my leg and gestured toward my drawing. "It's an image."

I looked down at it. "Yep."

"No, it's, you know, like a picture."

Her meaning sank in. "Brooke, I drew this. I can't go into something I've drawn."

"So, you've tried?" she asked, her tone challenging.

"Well, no, but only because it's ludicrous."

"How do you know?" She drew her legs underneath her and leaned toward me. "How do you know until you try?"

I knew that look. There was no getting past this. Until I gave it a try, there'd be no living with her. "Fine," I said, letting exasperation filter into my voice.

"What?" Kenya asked.

Cameron had settled onto the window seat and Jared sat on the floor beside me, scrolling through the pictures on my phone, his shoulder against my knee.

"She doesn't know?" Brooklyn asked me.

Glitch spoke up then, happy to fill her in. "Lor can go into pictures and see what happened when they were being taken. It's part of her superpowers."

Superpowers. If only.

"Wow. Okay," Kenya said, folding her arms across her chest. "That's cool."

"But I can't go into drawings."

"No," Brooklyn said, folding her arms across her chest as well, "you don't know that. Try."

After rolling my eyes so far back into my head, I almost fell backwards, I refocused on the drawing I'd done. It was disproportionate. The eyes too wide-set. The nose not quite centered. "I don't think this will work."

"You didn't think the other would work either. Concentrate."

I scanned the room. Brooke and Glitch looked on expectantly. Kenya curiously. And Jared humorously. Even Cameron seemed interested. "There's way too much pressure. You guys have to stop looking at me. I can't do this if you're looking at me."

Suddenly every gaze in the room had someplace else to be. It was silly. And it didn't help. I would never be able to do this. My shoulders sagged in defeat until Jared looked up at me and winked, his dark eyes sparkling with mirth. That one gesture, that one act of kindness, made me feel like I could do anything. Or at least give it my best shot.

I filled my lungs to capacity and laid my fingers across the page. Let them slide along the image. I focused on the primitive lines and the adolescent shading, and relaxed my body so it could fall through space and time. Not expecting much, I flinched when I felt something tremble beneath my touch. It surprised me and I snapped my hand back.

Thankfully, my guests were still minding their own business. Brooke was examining her nails. Kenya was cleaning hers with her switchblade. Glitch was playing *Asteroids* on my computer. Cameron was playing with his shoelaces and Jared was back to scrolling through my pictures.

I stared at the image again. The drawing was so rudimentary, surely I couldn't do something like go into it. Not in the same way I could a picture. I'd been going into them for weeks now, looking into a time past, seeing what was happening when the picture was taken, swimming through the moments it captured, but that was different. It was a photograph, a true copy of reality. This was nothing more than scribbles on paper.

"Well?" Brooke asked, her impatience shining through.

I tossed the drawing onto my desk. "Nothing. Just as I thought."

"Well, darn," she said, biting a nail to the quick. "This plan sucks."

"What plan?" I asked.

"Exactly."

THE WARM FUZZIES

I listened to the sound of my best friends breathing as they slept. I could tell everyone was unconscious except Cameron. He sat at the window seat, looking into the darkness.

Since it was just us, I decided to look through the journal my grandmother Olivia had taken from the nephilim again. Just as before, I saw nothing to indicate it was anything more than an ordinary sketchbook. It was full of drawings, mostly abstracts of people or still lifes. Some I could make out. Some I couldn't.

"You don't sleep much, do you?" I asked Cameron.

"Not really," he said, refusing to look my way.

"Well, I can't sleep, either. I'm going to get some water. Want anything?"

"Nope."

I wrestled my sheets down and climbed out of bed. He was sitting close to Brooke. Her bed was right by the window, so he had little choice, but in the moonlight, I could see his hand resting on her pillow, mere inches from her head as she slept. His thumb stroked a lock of her dark hair absently. He had pretty much everyone in town fooled, but not me. He had genuine feelings for Brooke. Probably had them for a long time. And it was me he was mad at, not her.

I tiptoed past Glitch, who was in his usual sleeping bag, and stepped right up to Cameron so I could whisper to him. He finally spared me a glance that was full of anger. Just as I thought.

I leaned in and he leaned back to get away from me.

"Not this time," I said. I leaned in farther and gave him a kiss on the cheek.

The next look he gave me almost made me laugh out loud. Confusion with a healthy side of horror had taken over.

I grinned and said, "Thank you for being everything that you are."

"I'm still mad at you."

"Exactly. Now get over it and tell Brooke how you feel."

He turned away. "She knows how I feel."

But he didn't see what I saw. He didn't realize that this was about as real as it was going to get. We were all about to die, and this little tiff between the two of them was an utterly useless waste of time.

I took his face into my hands and drew his gaze back to

mine. "No matter what happens," I said, fighting back the emotion that suddenly took hold, "I appreciate everything that you've done for me. And for Brooke."

"Yeah, no problem," he said, wary.

"Cameron, I love you. And, if you ever want to make out with me, you know like after school tomorrow, just let me know."

"Lorelei McAlister!"

I startled and turned toward Brooklyn, who had bolted upright on her bed. Her breathing had quickened when I stepped over and I knew she was awake. How could I let my last fleeting chances to punk her go to waste? We didn't have much time left, and I'd wasted a lot of that time in Maine with no one to harass. I had to get the jabs in while I could.

"What?" I asked, blinking in innocence. "You clearly don't want to make out with him. And, you know—" I gestured toward his general physique. "—he's kind of hot in a weird, nephilim sort of way."

Brooke bit down, fighting her natural instinct to sharpen her claws on human flesh, and slammed a fist into her pillow before throwing herself back onto it. "It's not going to work."

"Brooklyn Prather. You act like I had ulterior motives for putting the moves on your man. Don't you know me at all?"

"Yes." She pulled the covers up and crossed her arms over them. "That's exactly why it's not going to work."

I shrugged at Cameron, who sat glaring at me. It gave me the warm fuzzies, knowing I could frazzle my friends so. As I headed downstairs for a glass of water, I wondered what I could do to Glitch. His fear of turtles came to mind. Where would one find a turtle in New Mexico in the middle of winter?

I contemplated that as I started down the stairs and heard voices coming from the kitchen. It was well past my grand-parents' bedtime, and I had every intention of telling them that until I realized the voices were not theirs.

"I'm just wondering what your role in all this is."

I stopped to listen. Eavesdropping was an ugly job, but someone had to do it.

"I wonder that myself sometimes."

Jared. Mac was talking to Jared. I inched down another step. The guy had ears like a wolf. Jared, not Mac.

"I mean, you aren't in any of the prophecies," Mac said.

"Neither are you," Jared countered.

A soft laugh filtered up to me. "You got me there, Your Grace."

I loved it when they called Jared, a true prince of heaven, Your Grace. He, however, did not.

"Jared's fine."

Yes, he was.

"Jared it is, but I still wonder about how you play into all of this."

"I was sent," Jared said. "That's all I know, but you can think of me as a defensive guardsman, here to tackle the obstacles that get in Lorelei's way."

"But you were initially sent to take her." Mac's voice hard-ened. It wasn't Jared's fault his job title was the Angel of Death. People took that stuff so personally.

"I was, yes, but I knew something didn't fit. I knew what she was the moment I saw her."

"And what was that?"

"The last prophet," he said, matter-of-fact. "A direct de-scendant of Arabeth. And I knew what she was destined to do."

"So you disobeyed your orders? You saved her instead of taking her?" Mac asked him.

"Yes. I disobeyed my orders. Why would the only person purported to save the world from a supernatural war be killed before she could accomplish such a feat? It wasn't right."

After a long pause, Mac said, "I didn't think you guys could do that."

"We can't."

"Well, I'm grateful either way. It's just—"

The voices stopped just when I was getting into the conversation. I eased closer, straining to hear every syllable.

"It's just you look at her with . . . something else."

I could almost hear the smile in Jared's voice when he answered. "That's because I feel something else. I'm in love with her."

I froze. Jared was in love? Jared was in love with me? I let my lids drift shut and reveled in the sound of those words.

When Mac didn't respond, Jared continued. "If it makes you feel better, we've been together for centuries."

My lids flew open. What did he mean by that?

"I'm not sure I understand."

Intrigued, I leaned closer still, easing over as far as I could until my foot slipped off the step.

Looking back, I couldn't say that I fell head over heels down the stairs, but it sure felt like it. My foot landed at an angle on the next step and then the rest of the staircase came up to meet me, one step after another until I crashed on the kitchen floor. Thankfully, I was in capri pj's and not a nightgown. It could have been so much worse.

"Lorelei!" Mac called. He jumped up to help me, but nothing was more bruised than my pride. Heat rose up my neck and over my face as Mac picked me up and brushed me off.

Jared grinned from behind him. "Been there long?"

I gritted my teeth. He'd heard me. Freaking wolf.

"No," I said, my brows squishing together. "I just came downstairs."

"You did indeed," he said before winking at me. For a potential boyfriend, he didn't seem very concerned about my well-being.

In fact, he'd been pretty calm since I got back. Too calm, maybe. Like he knew something we didn't.

"You okay, Pix?" Mac asked.

I gave him my attention, loving the sound of my nickname on his voice. "I'm okay. Thanks."

Mac led me to a chair beside Jared. They'd been sitting at our tiny kitchen table. Mac was drinking coffee while Jared sipped on an orange soda. That would be my influence. I took the can from him and took a sip myself.

"So, what were you guys talking about?"

"You," Jared said without missing a beat.

"Yes, Jared was just telling me how long you two have known each other."

"A few months," he said to Mac before challenging me with his eyes. I could hardly argue about what I'd just heard without giving away the fact that I was indeed eavesdropping.

"Yep." I offered a congenial nod. "A few months."

In all honesty, I could have named the exact days, hours, and minutes since our first meeting in the halls of Riley High, but that seemed unnecessary.

With my sudden appearance, the conversation took on a whole new direction. Clearly Mac didn't want to question Jared's intentions in front of me. But I sure wanted him to. What were his intentions? What would happen to him when we were all dead and buried? Could I still see him? Could we date in heaven?

So many questions, so little time.

Mac seemed hesitant to leave us alone, so after about half an hour of idle chitchat that included things like the forming of the earth and stars and that whole book of Revelations thing, my lids started to droop.

"Bedtime," Jared said to me.

I snapped back to attention. "I'm fine."

"You're falling asleep at the table."

I rubbed my eyes. "No, I'm not."

"You're drooling," he added.

My hand shot to my mouth before I could stop it. I pressed my lips together. "I am not. I'm perfectly awake."

The skeptical grin he bestowed upon me was a thing of absolute beauty. I stilled and took it in before he said, "How about I take you upstairs."

"Um," Mac said, interrupting, "how about *I* take you upstairs?"

Jared laughed, the sound deep and husky. "Fair enough. Wait, what's that?" he asked, pointing toward the back of the house.

Mac turned to look, just as I did, but as I did so, Jared turned and put his mouth on mine so quickly, so softly, the kiss was only a brush of our lips before he pulled back and refocused on the back of the house again.

"What?" Mac asked.

My chest filled with such joy, such elation, that containing it when Mac turned back to us was like trying to block out the sun. But I did my best. I frowned and said, "I don't see anything, either." I even furrowed my brows as I looked past them. "Then again, I'm not a supernatural being."

———

I kissed Mac good night for the second time that night, closed the door to my bedroom, turned, and ran right into Jared. When I sucked in a startled breath, he covered my mouth with his hand and put an index finger over his lips to quiet me, gesturing with a nod of his head toward a departing Mac.

After waiting a moment for my paternal grandfather to get down the stairs, I pulled his hand from my mouth and looked up at the handsome boy standing before me. He did that. Appeared out of nowhere. I liked that about him.

He grinned and slid a lock of my hair through his fingers.

"You seem so different," I said. "So, I don't know, at ease with all this."

He rubbed the lock of hair over his mouth. "I've learned what it's like to live without you these past weeks. It's not a lesson I wish to repeat."

"Me neither, I can assure you, but that still doesn't explain why you suddenly seem to be taking all this really well."

"Humans are unpredictable," he said, walking backwards toward my bed and pulling me with him.

"I could've told you that."

"All this time I was worried about how we were going to do this. What was going to happen to the world? How could we possibly win?"

"I've had similar thoughts. Quite a few, in fact."

"But that's just it. I don't have to worry about it. Humans are unpredictable. Prophecies are not. So even though you believe with all your heart you're going to fail, failure—" He looked up in thought. "How do they say it in the movies?" After a second, he fixed a mirthful grin on me. "Failure is not an option."

"Been watching a lot of movies lately?"

He sat on my bed and literally pulled me into a straddling position onto his lap. I laughed and wrapped my arms around his wide shoulders. He felt heavenly. So much like a regular boy. Only with superpowers. And the ability to kill people with a touch.

"How is failure not an option?" I asked after settling in. "Because it feels pretty optional right now."

"It's written." He pulled me closer so he could nuzzle my neck. Goose bumps raced across my skin and I looked around, worried about our audience. "And they're asleep," he added.

He would know. I relaxed and reveled in the feel of him in my arms. I'd yearned for this moment for so long, I had to force myself to believe it was real.

"Thanks for coming to see me," he mumbled from the crook of my neck. His warm breath fanned over my collarbone.

"Coming to see you?"

"Mmm, the day I came for Elliot Davis."

He was referring to my visits, my delving inside the picture I had of him from the '70s.

I leaned back and gazed at him in astonishment. "You knew I would leave Riley's Switch. You knew I'd be gone, didn't you? I mean, I went inside the picture only recently, but for you it must have happened over forty years ago."

"It did, yes. And I did." His brows furrowed. "It's weird how things happen. How I've known you for only a microsecond in the grand scheme of things and yet forever." He looked down at me. "I've known you for a very, very long time. Even longer than you think."

"Is that what you meant when you told Mac we've been seeing each other for centuries?"

"It's related, yes."

I pressed my lips together in thought. "I don't understand."

But I'd lost him. He developed a sudden myopic interest in my wrist. Of all things. He took hold of it, lifted it to his mouth, grazed his teeth along the underneath. My pulse quickened in response.

"They weren't kidding when they said you'd be the most powerful prophet of them all."

I fought to stay alert, but his full mouth pressed against the inside of my wrist was just so—"Wait, they said that? Who are they?"

"The prophets that came before you. Even Arabeth's daughter, the one from your direct line, Lara Beth, prophesied that you, the last prophet, would be the most powerful of them all. And she was right. The more you learn, the more the past changes."

"What past?" I straightened. "Our past?"

"Yes." He trailed tiny kisses up the underside of my arm to the tender flesh inside my elbow, causing the most exquisite quakes to lace through my body and down my spine. "And because of that, we've known each other for a very, very long time."

"But how? I still don't understand."

"You will. When the time comes, you'll understand everything. There are things you have yet to discover about yourself. Powers you have yet to unleash."

"Like the power to resist you?" I asked, finding pleasure in his explorations, his touch, and the sound of his voice.

He laughed softly from behind a kiss at the crook of my elbow. "I hope not."

I laughed out loud, then quickly stopped myself, looking around at my slumbering guests.

He lifted his head, his eyes sparkling with appreciation, and gestured behind me. "Your grandfather's back."

I turned toward the door as Mac spoke rather loudly from the other side.

"Don't think for a minute I don't know you're in there, *Azrael.*"

Cameron jerked awake as I marveled at the brusqueness in my grandfather's tone, making a mental note never to make him angry. He'd said Jared's celestial name accusingly. Threateningly.

I rolled my eyes. "Angel of Death, Mac. Remember, he can kill you with a single touch? And you used a double negative."

"I'm going to use more than that if the only being in this house who is older than dirt doesn't stop pawing at my sixteen-year-old granddaughter."

Brooklyn stirred, felt blindly for Cameron's hand, then held it to her as she fell back into oblivion.

"I guess I should go," Jared said, laughing softly.

"I guess." Disappointment so palpable I could taste it sucked the happiness right out of my marrow.

"I'm waiting," Mac said.

I cringed. "I don't know about this whole two-grandfathers thing."

The next morning was like old times. Brooke and I got ready for school as Glitch ran home for a shower and fresh clothes and Cameron . . . did whatever it was Cameron did. We weren't sure, exactly. But it was nice having some time with Brooke. Almost alone. We still had Kenya to deal with, but she was fun to ignore. Then she spoke. Darn it.

"So, what's the deal with Glitch?" she asked through a wall of toothpaste.

"What do you mean?" I was towel-drying my hair, and Brooke was taking her turn in the shower.

"Is he seeing anyone?"

Brooke pulled the curtain aside to join me while I gawked at her. "Well, I'm not really sure. I know the twins are gone. Their family left when everyone else split, but—" I glanced askance at Brooke. "—is he seeing Ashlee? They seemed to be getting along really well when I left."

After a solid minute of Brooke staring Kenya up and down, she said, "Yeah. He's seeing someone. Or, well, okay." She shut the curtain. "I'm not really sure. I mean, they seem to like each other, but it didn't seem to be getting anywhere."

"I was really hoping that would work out. What was the problem?" I asked.

"Um, I'll give you a hint. His initials are Glitch Blue-Spider."

"Oh, yeah, that makes sense."

Kenya rinsed, then spit. "So, he may or may not be available."

Again, Brooklyn pulled the curtain aside to gawk. "Seriously? You and Glitch?" She eyed her up and down. "I don't see it. Sorry."

Kenya smirked at her. Oh, yeah, this was going to be a great day.

"I still think I should get the day off of school," I said, whining for the thousandth time. "I just got back. And the world is about to end. If ever I had a reason to ditch school."

"No way," Brooke said. "You have got to see what is going on. I mean the school is almost barren. Of the parents who didn't hightail it at the first sign of the apocalypse—which, by the way, how does one outrun an apocalypse?—half of those are keeping their kids at home. Either that or they changed their minds and are running after all. It's crazy."

"All because of a couple of storms and a few demon possessions?"

"Yep. But you haven't seen it. Remember Mr. Rivera? Juan's dad?" Before I could answer, she said, "He now walks around like a zombie. Oh, and so does Mrs. Long—only she actually looks like one, too."

"She always walked around like a zombie," I argued.

"Not like this. People in town are getting possessed left and right, and Jared is having to . . . I'm not sure what he does. Dispossesses them?"

"Cameron had talked about that before. Rats leaving a sinking ship. They want off this planet, off this plane, and they are committing spiritual suicide to do it by having Jared swallow them, having him breathe them into a place from which there is no return."

"But I thought having the world full of supernatural entities would be a good thing for other spirits," Kenya said.

"Not ghosts," Brooke replied, turning off the water as Kenya pulled her hair back, completely hogging the mirror. "According to Cameron, these are actually good ghosts who don't want to see the world destroyed or are afraid of what will become of them."

"When Jared first showed up," I explained further, "there was a poltergeist that was afraid of him. The mere thought floored me."

"It floored all of us," Brooke agreed. "The fact that spiritual entities could be afraid of one another. Could even go to war. It was not something that we absorbed overnight. It took a while."

"I think I'm still trying to absorb it all," I said.

"As for school," Brooke said as she stepped out of the shower, wrapped in a towel. "I just think, and your grandparents agree, that you might get an idea if you are out and about. We'll be like spies, looking for clues to a mystery."

"That would be sleuths."

"Either way."

"Brooke," I said, taking her aside. "I saw the end of the world a few days ago. I don't want to see it again. I don't want to touch anyone. Sometimes I can stop it, but if I'm distracted—"

"Oh, I totally have that covered. You just wear your coat and gloves the entire time."

"Won't that look odd?"

"Ha. Wait till we get to school. You'll understand."

We dressed and headed downstairs. Grandma had made breakfast, seeming more cheerful than usual, and we ate as we waited for Cameron to get back. Angry or not, he was our ride to school.

"You kids have a good day," Grandma said as we headed out.

Brooke threw her backpack over her shoulder and said quietly, "I haven't seen your grandmother this happy in weeks."

"Thanks for keeping an eye on them," I said to her.

"No prob. You guys always have food, so it was like getting paid in calories."

OUTSIDE OBSERVER

Jared met us at school, winding through throngs of reporters as they tried to interview us. He took my hand into his and threaded us through the melee while they asked us if we'd had any experiences with ghosts.

In a rare public appearance, Cameron walked up to one of the reporters, towered over him for a minute, then said quietly, "We are ghosts."

That stunned them into silence.

We walked into my old alma mater, and I realized

instantly Brooke hadn't been kidding. The halls were only half as full as usual. Teachers looked haggard, unkempt. Even the custodians watched all the students with a wary eye, as though worried we'd attack them. The entire atmosphere had a somber feel to it.

Brooke took Kenya to the office for a pass. She miraculously would have every class with me. The sheriff had called Mr. Davis the night before and arranged everything.

Jared excused himself, so I waited outside the office and wallowed in self-pity—it seemed like the right thing to do— until I saw Jared pull a girl in between the walls of lockers. I stepped over and peeked around. It was the same girl I'd seen yesterday, the one standing on the street, staring at us as we passed. No, staring at Jared.

She had stringy blond hair and bloodshot eyes above dark circles that made them look twice as big as they were.

"You'll not come back from this," he said to her.

She kept her head down but looked up at him from underneath her lashes. "I understand, Azrael. I want off before it begins."

She was possessed, and the soul inside her wanted off the plane before the war started. Clearly it knew something no one else did. Or something everyone else was refusing to see.

Jared wrapper his fingers around her jaw, his large hand covering half her face. Then he bent down and angled his head as though to kiss her, covering his mouth with hers. Even though I knew what they were doing, my heart seized just a little as I watched the exchange. He pulled back and breathed in the possessing spirit. A darkness left her mouth and entered his until she was emptied of the unwanted presence. Her eyes rolled back instantly and she collapsed into his arms.

He turned to me as he scooped her up into his arms, his chivalry one of the sexiest things I'd ever seen.

"I have to get her to the nurse's office," he said, starting that way.

I nodded, no longer even a little jealous. He was doing a job. His job. And that made him noble. He carried her swiftly into the south hall and I leaned against the lockers, utterly in awe of him.

Hearing a familiar footstep, I looked over and saw Ms. Mullins walking toward her classroom. Every molecule in my body brightened. She was my favorite teacher and, as we'd only recently found out, the observer, the person sent to keep an eye on us, the Order of Sanctity and me. The question was, sent from where?

I rushed up to her and she flashed a smile that could melt the polar ice caps. She had dark cropped hair and sparkling blue eyes that made her look like she was forever up to mischief.

A little shaky after what I'd just witnessed, I said breathily, "Hi, Ms. Mullins."

She tsked and pulled me into a hug. "And she returns at last," she said, positively beaming. "I'm so glad you're back."

"I'm so glad to be back." I leaned in to her. "But what about the other thing. I mean, your other position?"

"I had to report that I'd been found out. They sent another."

"Who is it?" I asked, intrigued.

"If I told you, he or she would have to report in that they had been compromised, and we'd have to start all over again. Besides, I have no idea."

Not too disappointed, I decided to pry just a bit further.

"Who sent you to observe in the first place? I mean, who even knows about us? About what's going on here?"

"I'm not supposed to tell, actually, but since—" A sadness fell over her. "Since it's all happening, really happening, I guess it can't hurt anything."

I inched closer to her. "And?"

"I'm an emissary of the Vatican."

If she'd hit me with a two-by-four, I would not have been more surprised. "The Vatican? Like the one in Vatican City?"

She laughed softly. "The very one."

I blinked. "But why?"

"We've been following the prophecies of the descendants of Arabeth for centuries. When you were born, well, we had to send someone, and I was chosen. It was a great honor."

I stepped back in astonishment. "I don't understand. I mean, if they've been studying the prophecies, too, do they know how to stop this war? Surely they know more than we do."

"They do know."

I straightened and waited expectantly.

"You."

Just as quickly, I deflated. "Don't tell me. It all hinges on me, and I'm going to stop this war before it even begins."

"That pretty much covers it."

Disappointment cut into me. "Ms. Mullins, I don't know how. I didn't know how yesterday and I still don't know how today."

"But you will."

"No! I won't. Everyone . . . everyone has such high hopes. I just don't know what to do." Tears burned my eyes. If any-one would understand, surely it was my favorite teacher. "Call them," I said, a new plan forming in my mind. "Call them and tell them the truth. Tell them I'm an idiot and I don't know what I'm doing and if they don't do something immediately, we're all going to die."

"Lorelei—"

"Please, Ms. Mullins. They have to know more. They have to tell me what to do."

She pulled me close. "Lorelei, we will get through this. You'll figure it out."

She was wrong. So very, very wrong. My last hope for information vanished into thin air. "Do they at least know who opened the gates in the first place?"

"No." Even she seemed disappointed with that. "They have no idea."

"Sadly, neither do we."

I walked to Ms. Mullins's class in a daze and feeling a little bipolar. One minute I was certain we'd figure it out; the next, I was just as certain we were all going to die screaming. I was tired and cold and hungry. No, wait, just tired. Since over half the class was gone, Ms. Mullins showed a video on the difference between fusion and fission while she, Brooklyn, and I chatted in the back of the room, setting a horrible example for the rest of the students. While we came to exactly zero conclusions, we did have a nice time.

After first hour, Brooke and I headed for the bathroom.

I opened the door with my hip while saying over my shoulder, "I bet we could be tardy to second and no one would care."

"Oh, they don't. Trust me. I'm tardy to almost every class now. The world has turned upside down." She said all this while checking under the stalls to make sure no one else was in the room. When the coast was clear, she said, "Okay, I have you alone at last, which, my God, is so much harder to accomplish than one might think." She put her backpack on the ground and stabbed me with one of her mom stares. "What happened last night when you touched your drawing?"

I shouldn't have been surprised that she'd seen my reaction. "You were supposed to be looking away."

"Whatever. What happened?"

"Nothing. Not a vision anyway, if that's what you want to hear."

"But something did happen, yes?"

"Yes. But it was, I don't know, a ripple."

She hitched a hip against a sink. "A ripple. Like in time? Like you were about to go into the drawing?"

"Not really. I don't know," I said, adding a childish whine to my voice. Why did we have to talk about this?

"Lorelei, you are the most powerful prophet in the line. Did you know that?"

"Jared told me last night. Did my grandparents find that written somewhere?" I asked, trying to change the subject.

"Yes, in lots of places. It's odd because as some of the prophecies come to pass, others make more sense. I'm not sure what it all means, but more than one of your ancestors said you'd be the most powerful of them all."

"I don't feel very powerful."

"I'm just saying, you should try that again. Maybe you can go into it. Maybe you didn't give it enough time."

"I gave it enough time."

"But maybe you didn't."

"But I did."

"But maybe—"

"Fine," I said, exasperated. I pulled out the sketch. "Would you like me to try it now?"

What was supposed to be a chastisement only served to

urge Brooke on. "Absolutely," she said, her eyes sparkling with anticipation.

"Maybe we can have a séance, too, right here in the girls' room."

"You think?" she asked, teasing me.

I opened the sketchbook to the picture I'd drawn and took off my gloves. "This is not my best work," I said to her.

She looked down at it. "In all fairness, you were six at the time."

"True."

After releasing a loud sigh to emphasize my annoyance, I settled onto the countertop and touched my fingertips to the picture. I concentrated on clearing my mind, relaxing my muscles, focusing on the lines, the blurriness of the man's face, the wind cutting through the air. Then I heard it. The wind. I felt it against my skin, and the ripple that had quaked through my fingertips before did so again.

A tightness wrapped around me as the wind roared around me, and my first thought was of my parents—the scene so real, I fought to breathe under the weight of it. I was back. I was at the ruins where my parents disappeared. It had been ten years, but I was there. I looked around frantically, wanting to see them, praying I'd see them, but they were already gone. I'd entered the scene too late. I looked on as a beast stood before me. He was as tall as the trees around us. His shoulders as wide as the horizon.

Fear gripped me so fast and so hard, I was catapulted out of the picture.

"Lorelei," Brooklyn said, her voice muffled as though she were underwater. "Lorelei, it's me."

I pushed at her, held out my arms to keep her back, kicked out. Then I realized where I was. I'd scrambled for a corner of the girls' restroom and found myself wedged between a wall and a trash can.

"Lor, are you okay?" Brooke's eyes were like saucers, wide and uncertain. "Lor," she said right before collapsing into my arms. "I thought you had a seizure or something."

"What happened?" I asked.

"You fell and flew back against the concrete."

That would explain the splitting headache I suddenly had.

"And your eyes rolled back. I thought— Oh, my God—"

"I'm okay," I said, soothing her, hugging her back. I realized then that Kenya had come in. She stood in the doorway, her expression wary.

"I did it," I said breathlessly. "I went into the drawing, and it was like I was there."

Brooke sat back, her hands still on my shoulders. "You went into it?"

I nodded. "But only for a second. It—it was horrible. It was so real. I remembered everything."

Brooke sank onto her bottom.

"Malak-Tuke. I saw him again. He was standing before a little girl."

"You," she corrected. "He was standing before you."

Kenya sat beside Brooke. The bell rang but we ignored it.

"Brooke," I said, "how is that even possible?"

"No," she said, thinking back. "It is. It's totally possible. I remember reading that one of Arabeth's daughters did something similar."

"Oh, yes," Kenya said, closing her eyes in thought. "My parents told me about it. She would draw pictures with ashes from certain herbs that she burned, and she could see into them. Into the pictures." She blinked in bewilderment. "This is just so cool. I can't wait to tell my parents."

"No," I said, suddenly self-conscious. "Not yet. What if I can't do it again? What if it means nothing?"

"Nothing?" she said. "Lorelei, this could be the answer. You have to tell your grandparents."

I curled my hands into fists and covered my eyes with them. I was so tired of being scared. So tired of feeling like a fraud. Of being told I was something I wasn't. That I would do something I couldn't. I had to get the bloody heck over myself and fast.

"Maybe you're right," I said, almost agreeing. "But first, let me see what else I can get from this picture."

"You're going back in?" Brooklyn asked, her eyes wide once more with fear. When I nodded, she said, "No way. Not yet. This time, we need backup."

We gathered the troops and called my grandparents on the way home.

"Okay, they're waiting for us in the basement at church." The basement was the Order of Sanctity's headquarters. It was where all the archives were stored. All the documents and texts that my father and his father and so on over the decades had collected. "They aren't going to be thrilled that we didn't tell them about this before," I said, suddenly worried.

"Here." Kenya held out her hand. "Take off your glove and check."

"Kenya, I don't want to see that again."

"But if this really is the answer, then things will have changed, right?"

Reluctantly, I did as she'd wanted. And she was right. Things had changed. Oh, her death was still brutal. She was scared, terrified beyond reason. Only this time, she died in Riley's Switch. She died a thousand miles away from her family, running for her life alone. No. I looked to the left. Running for me. Trying, even in her last moments on earth, to protect me. My despair knew no bounds. That this beautiful girl would die on my account.

When I came out of the vision, tears burned my eyes. I clenched my jaw to fight them and looked out the window. "Nothing has changed," I said, my throat raw.

I could feel her disappointment.

"I'm sorry," I said, wanting to curl into a ball and sleep for a thousand years. "I wish I were better at this stuff."

Kenya scoffed. "You're amazing," she said. "You have no idea. If I could do half the stuff you can, I'd be thrilled."

"You must think I'm pretty unappreciative."

"You are."

"But you've known about me your whole life," I argued, suddenly defensive. "Do you know how long I've known about me?"

She quirked a brow. "Since you were born?"

"No. Well, yes, but not *me*. *Me*-me. The prophet me."

"How long?"

"About four months. That's it. And I only found out after I was hit by a huge green delivery truck and was slated to die only to have the Angel of Death swoop down and save me."

She nodded. "Oh, yeah, I'd wallow in a constant state of self-pity, too." She did that deadpan thing she was so fond of. "You forget. I've seen the Angel of Death. The Angel of Death is hotter than a two-dollar pistol. That must have been a real hardship."

She totally didn't understand.

We got to the church and entered through the back door, winding our way down the small staircase to the basement underneath. I wasn't sure whom all Granddad had called, but it seemed like we had a pretty full house. Besides my grandparents and Mac, the sheriff was there as well as a few elder members of the Order. I could've killed Brooklyn.

"What the heck did you tell my granddad?"

"That we had a Code Three emergency."

"What's a Code Three emergency?"

"No idea, but it got his attention. He said to meet us here."

I didn't know whether to admire her or worry.

"Okay," Granddad said gravely. "Whatever happened, we can figure it out together. So, what happened?"

They were sitting in the boardroom at a large table they used for meetings, research, and lively discussions on the logistics of the prophecies. We took seats around the room as well and I faced my grandfather head-on.

"There's something I never told you," I said, wondering how they would take it. I figured Mac would understand my reasons for not mentioning it sooner. Or I hoped so. "I can see into pictures."

They sat there with blank stares as though waiting for the punch line.

"No, like pictures. Photographs. I can see into them."

Grandma spoke up first. "We aren't sure what you mean, sweetheart."

"She can go into them," Brooke said, taking over for me. "She can look at a picture, concentrate, and go into it. She can see what was happening when it was taken. But that's not why we're here."

"Nope," Glitch said. "She can do something much cooler than that."

"She can draw a picture and go into that as well," Kenya said, joining in. She seemed way too excited by the prospect.

Mac scrubbed his stubbly jaw and was about to say something when Kenya interrupted.

"Like that other prophet, one of Lara Beth's daughters. She would draw pictures with the ashes of special herbs she'd burned and go into them. Remember? That's how she got her visions."

My grandparents nodded as well as a couple of the church elders.

Mac finally got a word in. A few, actually. "No one has been able to do that for centuries," he said. "That's an incredible gift."

All in all, they seemed to take it well.

"Pix," Granddad said, "why didn't you tell us this before?"

"I don't know. It just seemed kind of a useless thing to be able to do."

"But wait!" Brooke said. She was way too happy, too. "There's more!" She nodded encouragingly. "Tell them."

I took a deep breath. "Okay, so I decided I'd try to remember more about the man that day, the one who opened the gates of hell the first time."

"Dyson," Grandma said. If only knowing that name helped. It got us nowhere fast.

"Yes, Dyson, if that's the same man. So I thought back to what he looked like and drew a picture."

Glitch got my backpack and pulled out the sketchbook

for me. He turned it to the sketch and handed it to Granddad.

"Well, Brooklyn had an idea, so we tried it."

"Right," she said, excited. "I figured if she could go into
pictures, she maybe could go into any kind of picture. Even
a drawing, you know? So she tried it and it didn't work the
first time but I knew she was holding something back because she does that so when we were in the restroom today I
told her I knew she was holding something back and she
said I'm not and I said I can tell you are and she said, okay,
maybe I am but I didn't go into it, and I said well you need
to try again and—"

"What Brooke is trying to say," I said, cutting her off so
she could supply her red blood cells with oxygen, "is that she
convinced me to try again."

Grandma's astonished expression turned hopeful. "And?"
she asked.

"And it worked." I lowered my head, suddenly uncertain.
"I was there again. I was back at that day."

Granddad touched my knee to draw me back to him.
"You went back to that day through your drawing?"

"Yes. It was not pleasant."

"She bumped her head," Brooke said, turning my near-
fatal concussion into a bump. "And it was scary because I
thought she was having a seizure or something."

Mac rushed to the archive room. We heard him rummaging around, then he hurried back with a stack of old
papers that were held together with a leather tie.

"I found it. Where Arabeth's daughter talks about how she
burned the herbs and scribed with the ashes. And if I remember correctly, she would go into a trancelike state. At first, her
family . . . Yes, here it is." He read a passage, then paraphrased

for us. "At first her family thought she was having seizures until they realized she was divining. She was prophesying through her own drawings." He looked up at me then. "And you can do the same thing." The pride in his eyes caused me to both feel good about what I could do and worry that they would all think this was the answer we'd all been waiting for.

Grandma clasped her hands over her heart and said, "This is the answer we've all been waiting for."

Nailed it. "But what if it's not?" I asked.

"I will put you in a headlock and scrub your scalp raw," Kenya said.

Everyone turned to her in surprise.

"What?" she asked, defensive. "She needs to get over herself, for the love of gravy. This is what she was destined for. What she is going to do. And she's so worried about letting us all down. It's ridiculous."

My temper flared. "Are you kidding me? Do you know what will happen if I do let you all down? The world is destroyed. Everyone dies. Excuse me if I'm feeling a little pressure here."

She smirked at me and leaned forward until we sat nose to nose. "If I were given this gift, I wouldn't act like a scared rabbit waiting to be boiled for dinner."

"Oh, yeah? What would you do, then? If this was on you, what would you do?"

"I'd fight. Until my dying breath, I'd fight for everyone I loved. I wouldn't run and hide under a rock and complain and turn all squirrely every time a new gift, a gift that most people would kill for, was handed to me on a silver platter."

Tears burned my eyes, because no matter how bad I hated to admit it, she was right. I was acting like such a monumental wuss.

"All you do is complain about how you have these visions and how hard they are."

"Okay, I got it."

"And you walk around all 'poor me.'"

"I said, I got it." My temper started to rise again.

"It's pathetic. You have no idea how fortunate you are to be able to do what you do. I know you lost your parents. I get it, but that is not on you. They died protecting you. Protecting all of us, and all you can do is whine about it. Quit acting like the world is—"

That was it. I lunged forward. Switchblade or not, Kenya Slater was going to eat cement if I had anything to say about it. Sadly, she was about twelve feet taller than I was, and God only knew how many pounds she had on me, so when I went to tackle her, I more or less gave her a really aggressive bear hug. But I'd surprised her.

"Pix!" Grandma said.

I'd knocked her off balance.

"I'm not sure this kind of behavior is called for."

We tumbled to the ground and, yes, like a girl, I went for the hair. I grabbed handfuls with the intent of banging her head against the concrete floor beneath us. But I did not factor in the fact that she actually knew how to fight. She was all martial arsty-fartsy and I had been in only one fight my entire life, and that was with a girl my own size. Brooklyn. We got into a catfight in the third grade, and as much as I hated to admit it, she kicked my ass.

"Bill," Grandma squeaked, "do something. This is quite uncalled for."

I quickly realized I didn't stand a chance. It hit me when she easily maneuvered over me and dragged an arm behind my back to hold me to the ground. But the one thing I had on my side was anger. Just because she'd wanted to be me her whole life and she would've loved to have the gifts I have didn't give her the right to talk about what it was like to be me. Or, more important, talk about my parents and what they had done.

I knew that all too well. I was there.

"Bill, really!"

I scrambled out from under her and brought my legs around until I had her head in a scissors hold. She clawed at my arm, then at my legs when I'd locked her down and tried to slam her head into the cement again. Before I could manage it, I rose into the air. I felt an arm around my waist as I was lifted up and back against a solid chest.

"Okay, Rocky," Jared said, the humor in his voice apparent.

But adrenaline was rushing through me at light speed. I swung my arms, trying to get another piece of her until he wrapped his other arm around mine. His mouth was at my ear then, warm and sensual when he whispered, "Do you want a spanking, young lady?"

I stilled instantly, the thought of the Angel of Death bending me over his knee causing a second wave of adrenaline, only in other areas.

Oh.

My.

God.

I was into BDSM.

He chuckled at my back.

"That was exciting!" Brooklyn said, her face flush with, well, excitement. "You were totally holding your own."

"Really?" I asked, surprised and feeling an odd sense of pride as Jared lowered me to the floor.

"Totally! Unlike the time I kicked your butt. You were pretty pathetic that time."

"Yeah, whatever. You sucker-punched me."

"Dude, I told you I was going to hit you."

"Yeah, but I thought you were just talking crap. I didn't expect you to follow through."

Kenya stood and brushed herself off. She turned to me, her chest swelling with something I hadn't expected. Pride. "Better," she said, a mischievous grin lighting her face. "Much, much better."

I would never figure that girl out.

"Now that the MMA exhibition fight is over," Mac said, one corner of his mouth twitching, "can we hear more about this new talent of yours?"

I looked around at everyone. My family. Members of the Order. My best friends on earth. Embarrassment rushed through me like a wildfire, scorching my insides. "Sorry," I said.

"Oh, no you don't." Kenya stood again, her stance aggressive. "Don't you dare run back to your hidey-hole."

"What are you talking about, Kenya?" I asked, becoming frustrated.

"You got spunk, girlfriend." She backhanded my arm in camaraderie. "Let it shine."

"You don't have to make fun of me."

"No, I mean it. That girl that just showed up? The one who tried to kick my ass? That's who you are. Deep down inside. And that's who you need to be if we are going to do this. So, chin up, Balboa."

NO PRESSURE

After things settled down, I explained exactly how I did what I did. Mac was worried about the possibility of an honest-to-goodness concussion, so Jared and Cameron brought out one of the cots we had set up in the archive room.

"She might have a concussion already," Brooke said. "She hit hard. Either her head split or the floor. Not sure which."

"Yeah, well, I'm not as hardheaded as you are. And by the feel of things, it was my head and not the floor."

"Then you gave it a run for its money, I can tell you that

much. Quite the combatant today," she added with a soft laugh.

Grandma lowered the lights a little as Jared took my hand and helped me lie down on the cot.

"I'm not sure I can do this with everyone standing around."

"Sure you can," Kenya said, excited about the prospect of watching.

"No, she's right," Granddad said.

"That's okay." Mr. Henderson waved a hand. "We'll go. Just let us know what you find out."

Mr. Henderson was one of the members furious with my grandparents for sending me away. I wasn't sure how to feel about him now. While I understood his misgivings on one level, I couldn't help but hold a certain amount of resentment toward him, toward all of those who gave my grandparents a hard time while I was gone. It was probably best that he leave.

Everyone except my family members and best friends left. Unfortunately, that did little to relieve my doubt.

"Okay, Pix, how's this?" Mac asked as he knelt beside me.

"Great. No pressure, right?"

He grinned that charming grin of his. "None at all. If this doesn't work, that's okay, honey."

Glitch handed me the sketchbook. "Good luck," he said. I nodded.

"You can do this," Brooke said. She took the seat that Grandma had set beside the cot.

Cameron stood at the foot of the cot while Jared stood at the head. I tilted my head back and looked at him. He winked at me. Even upside down, that guy could stop a heart with one grin. Actually, he probably *could* stop a heart with one grin, since that was his job and all. He was so handsome, though. So magnificent. God took his time on that one.

"We'll be right here," he said.

They were there for a reason. If I did have a seizure or whatever it was that happened before, my grandparents didn't want me getting hurt, so I had bodyguards of a sort.

Nervousness tingled inside me as I took the sketch and looked it over again. It really was rudimentary. Embarrassment washed through me for the umpteenth time, and I realized Kenya was right. I really needed to get over myself.

I siphoned cool air in through my nose and out through my mouth in concentration. I needed to go further back this time. I wanted to see my parents. Or not. This was the most painful day of my existence. The day they disappeared. Did I really want to see that again?

Just getting into the picture would be hard enough. I decided to leave it at that. To just do my best. After one last look at Mac, who was still kneeled beside me, I touched the image. It was cool beneath my fingers. The texture of the drawing paper almost rough. I focused, relaxed my eyes until the lines I'd drawn merged into a blur. Then I closed my eyes. And I waited. And waited. This time there was no wind. No roaring or whipping of dirt in the air.

"I don't think it worked," I said, opening my eyes.

The room had brightened and I blinked as Grandma turned the lights back up. But it wasn't Grandma. It was the sun. I was outside. I was at the ruins where my parents had disappeared.

Startled, I looked up and saw the demon again, its shoulders blocking out a good portion of the afternoon sky. I bit down, tried not to let my fear catapult me out of the picture this time. If he was already here, that would mean that my parents were already gone. I looked around for them frantically anyway, but all I saw was a little girl staring up at the demon. Her curly red hair stuck out in all the wrong places. Her tiny hands curled into fists as she looked up at the beast. At Malak-Tuke. And just like Kenya said, I stood my ground. I was only six years old, but I was ready to fight the demon until my dying breath. If only I still had that sense of bravado. That bravery that only innocence brings.

He looked down at the girl, at me, and I saw things I didn't see back then. His claws were razor sharp and as long as my legs. He perched one under my chin and lifted my face to his. I didn't remember that. I never remembered that one act of . . . humanity?

But all the feelings I remembered, the fear, the adrenaline coursing through my veins, were there. I could feel them all over again. Just like I felt what others felt when I had visions, I felt my own emotions rise up and choke me. I was both feeling them anew and reliving what had already happened, what was branded into my mind like an insignia. So the emotions that coursed through me now were twofold.

I stood with my fists at the ready, my face puckered in a combination of fear, anger, and determination. Malak-Tuke slid another of his claws along my cheek and over my jawline. Then, just like I did remember, he dematerialized. He became smoke and mist and entered my mouth, burrowed into my lungs, curled around my spine.

I both remembered and felt anew the acidic texture of him as I breathed him in. His essence scorched my throat and seized my lungs until I stopped fighting for air and accepted him.

And we became one.

"No!"

We turned and watched as a man ran toward us. Dyson. I didn't know it at the time, but this was Dyson.

"No!" he yelled. "I summoned you, not her!"

He fell to his knees in front of us. Grabbed my shoulders. Shook me. His impudence would not go unpunished. He was screaming in our face and we didn't like it.

He was screaming in our face.

I moved closer to the scene, watched like a voyeur as the man who opened the gates of hell shook me. That was so wrong. I was only six.

I suddenly realized I was outside myself again, looking on. I moved even closer, knelt down beside myself to get a better look at the man as the little-girl me scanned the ground around her and I remembered, we'd picked up a stick and stabbed him. It was his own fault. He was screaming in our face.

She spotted a stick, the stick I remembered picking up, the same crooked piece of wood, the same jagged edges, only she stopped. And looked at me.

This didn't happen before. I never stopped and looked at anything. I picked up that stick—we picked up that stick— and stabbed him without regard for anything other than con-vincing him to go away. But she stopped and I peered into my own gray eyes. Red curls hung over them, partly obscuring her vision, but she stared into my eyes with a knowing far beyond her six years.

She raised a hand to my cheek, and a darkness drifted out of her. Malak-Tuke's essence wafted around her like a dark fog. I could see it, something I'd never seen before. It was both fascinating and horrific. But I could also see what I as-sumed was her aura. My aura. And it was just like Jared had described. Fire licked over my skin and danced around me, bathed me in a soft glow.

I wondered if this was what fascinated Malak-Tuke. The fire that had been passed down from Arabeth, through generations of prophetic women. It was the fire Arabeth had been burned in. She used it, absorbed it, transformed it into a positive thing before she died. And she sent it to her three daughters, one of whom was my direct ancestor.

The little-girl me raised a hand to my cheek. "You can do this," she said.

"What?" The man beside us was still screaming. Still shaking us.

Then his face morphed from anger into shock. He looked down at the stick protruding from his abdomen, and recognition shot through me. I knew him.

"You can do this, Lorelei!"

I swallowed huge gulps of air as I was catapulted once again out of the picture and back to reality.

"You can do this."

It was my grandmother's voice. She was frightened, her voice quivering as she kept hold of my forearm.

Then I realized other hands were on me as well. I was being held down by several people. Jared was holding my head. Cameron my feet. And Mac and Granddad were draped across my body. At that moment I realized I was thrashing about. Catching only brief glimpses of those around me. Brooklyn's hands were over her mouth, her eyes wide with horror.

Wonderful. What'd I do now?

Grandma was helping Granddad. Or trying to.

"What?" I asked, only it came out more like a gurgle. That was embarrassing.

My muscles strained against my skin as though trying to break free of it. They ached instantly, and I tried to force myself to relax.

"She's coming out of it."

I'm already out of it. I've been out of it. But my body wouldn't obey. It wanted to thrash about a little more for good measure.

I tried again to make myself relax, to slow my racing heart. Then I remembered what I had to tell them and my heart sped up again.

"I know him!" I said, and it kind of sounded right.

"Lorelei," Grandma said. "We called an ambulance."

A what? "No, I'm okay, I saw him. I recognized him."

"Don't try to talk, baby," Mac said at my side. "The ambulance will be here soon."

I took Jared's hand in mine. "I'm okay. I don't need an ambulance. I have to tell you what I saw."

"Can you drink?" Grandma asked. She held out a cup of water from the dispenser.

Jared helped me into a sitting position, but I collapsed back against him. He sat on the cot and braced me against his chest, holding my head in his strong hands.

"I saw him," I said again.

Grandma held the cup to my mouth. Why were they not listening to me?

"I saw the man. I saw Dyson." With those words, I realized I was slurring a bit. I tried again to force myself back, taking a sip of water as the world tipped a little to the left. "I'm okay," I said, my breaths ragged. "I feel like I just ran a marathon, though."

A round of nervous laughter filled the area as Grandma sat beside me. She took my face into her hands. "Lorelei. Oh, heavens, Lorelei." She kissed both of my cheeks and my mouth before placing the cup at my lips again.

"What happened?" I asked after taking another sip.

Sirens filtered down the stairs.

"You had a seizure," Brooklyn said, her voice soft, her face pale. "Let's not do that anymore, okay?"

I saw Glitch then. He was crouching down in a corner, his arms crossed over his chest. Kenya was close by him.

"I guess going into drawings is different than going into pictures. But I'm fine," I said, glancing from one person to another until my gaze landed on Granddad's. "I don't need an ambulance."

Grandma felt my cheeks as though checking for a fever. "That was the scariest thing I've ever seen," she said, her eyes bright with moisture.

"Really?" I asked, feeling an odd sense of mirth. "That's what you said when that bear got into the store that one time."

She closed her eyes in relief. "That was scary. This was horrifying."

"Wait, why? Did I look bad?" My hand shot to my mouth. "Did I drool?"

Glitch hurried up the steps then right back down, ushering an EMT into the room. He took one look at us, probably took in the fact that we were in a nondenominational church, and frowned. "What's going on?" he asked as he walked over to my side.

Before I could answer, Kenya said, "Well, McAlister here was having a seizure, and instead of taking her to the hospital, we decided to pray over her until she was healed." She beamed at me. "It totally worked!"

I laughed, but Granddad didn't seem to find it amusing. He raked a hand down his face as Sheriff Villanueva burst into the room, summed up the situation with a once-over, then took the EMT aside to assure him my family was not risking my welfare by refusing to take me to the hospital.

"We're the ones who called you," Granddad said.

I patted his arm and stood to convince the EMT I was okay. Or, well, I attempted to stand. Jared stood first to help me to my wobbly feet. "I'm fine," I said to the man as his partner walked into the room. "I wasn't feeling well, so I lay down and they called you. I'm sorry, but I'm okay now. Really. I did not have a seizure."

"The hell you didn't," Cameron said.

I ground my teeth and glared at him. "I'm fine and we—" I circled my index finger around the room, indicating all those present. "—need to talk."

"About what?" he asked, challenging me.

Did they really not understand a word I said earlier? Fine. They brought this on themselves. "About the fact that I recognized the man who opened the gates of hell ten years ago."

Everyone stilled. Even the EMTs.

Mac recovered first. "Kids," he said to the men, shaking his head in a helpless gesture. "The things that come out of their mouths."

Granddad was next. "Yes, and we're sorry about this. She's better."

"Yeah," Brooklyn said. "This kind of thing happens all the time. She has these mental issues."

"Brooke!"

"What?" she asked, pressing her mouth together. "Like you don't."

"Like *you* don't."

"Not as bad as you."

"Puh-lease."

"Girls," Grandma said. "Is this really the time?"

We started to argue. We were quite in the moment, but when we saw Grandma's expression, the one urging us to focus on what was important, we glanced at each other, and then, as dutiful granddaughters should, we hung our heads in shame.

"Sorry," I said, punching Brooke on the arm.

She elbowed me back. It felt good, horsing around with her again. It had been too long. But Grandma was right. We needed to focus on the important issues at the moment. Not the fact that I wanted to horse around with my best friend.

"I guess we're done here," the EMT said. He gave me a warning glare before turning to leave.

"These people are freaks," his partner said as they ascended the stairs. "All the crap going on in this town is bringing out the crazies."

Brooke jammed her fists onto her hips. "That was rude."

"Completely," I agreed. "And really? Mental issues?"

She tossed me a saucy smirk as Jared helped me sit down before I collapsed. Whatever happened had sapped my energy, but his grip was sure, strong. I found myself wanting to collapse against him again. I liked being collapsed against him.

The sheriff came back in after seeing the EMTs out. He pulled up a chair and everyone sat back down.

"Okay, Pix," Granddad said, "what did you see?"

I lowered my head. "I didn't see Mom and Dad. I really wanted to, but I arrived in the scene after they were already gone."

Jared had sat back on the cot with me and had pulled me against him and wrapped his arms around my shoulders. My sudden weakness was a great excuse for him to do so. He offered me a consoling squeeze.

"But you were there?" Grandma asked, still in awe of the whole thing.

"I was. I went inside a drawing."

"But again," Brooke said, "I vote we don't do that any-more, for the record."

I wanted to laugh out loud. Brooke. The one who'd been pushing me relentlessly ever since we found out about my *gift,* and here she was voting it down. I owed it to myself to retaliate. I didn't need my gift to tell me she was going to get a whole lot of ribbing in her near future.

But still. "Why would going into an image affect me that way?"

"I think it affected your ancestor the same way," Mac said.

"What was it like, Pix," Grandma asked.

"It was very similar to when I go into a picture, only ap-parently much more physically demanding. I'm just there, Grandma. I can just see everything that's going on. And I saw things I didn't remember. Like Malak-Tuke touching my face before he dematerialized. And I saw me like you see me," I said to Jared. Then to Cameron. "I think I saw my aura as a little girl."

Jared brushed a lock of hair off my cheek. Another great excuse. "Was it like fire? Bright and luminous?"

"Exactly."

Cameron stepped back. "You did see it. That's exactly— I mean—"

"I know. It freaked me out, too."

"And you saw him?" Mac asked. "You saw the man?"

"I did. Oh! Yes, I did! And I recognized him!"

Grandma fixed a hopeful expression on Granddad.

"Who was it, Pix?" he asked.

"I have no idea."

After a stunned moment of silence, he said, "What?"

I shrank back in disappointment. "I'm so sorry. I recognize

him, but I can't place why. He's someone I know or someone I see semi-regularly. I know I've seen him recently."

"Can you describe him?" Cameron asked.

"Light brown hair, almost blond, light eyes, medium-ish build. He's kind of thin but not athletic looking. He looked like he worked in an office or something. And he was wearing a light blue button-down shirt, again, like he worked in an office."

"Maybe he's an insurance salesman," Brooke said, and we all questioned her with raised brows. "I mean, my dad's insurance guy wears button-downs all the time."

If the situation weren't so dire, I would've laughed. Brooke logic. There was nothing more entertaining.

"Okay," Cameron said, "maybe we can do something to jar your memory."

"Like electroshock therapy?"

This time the look we placed on Brooke was full of horror instead of humor. "Seriously, Brooke?" I asked, appalled.

"Right, right. That wouldn't help. Sorry, that whole seizure thing threw me off my game."

I couldn't stop myself. She was still sitting in a chair beside me. I leaned over and hugged her. "It's like having my very own fruitcake."

She patted my back. Really hard.

PIZZA AND SUBS

We spent the rest of the afternoon trying to jar my memory, thankfully without the use of electroshock therapy. If we knew who this guy was, surely we could stop him from trying to open the gates again. I drew another picture of him, but this one wasn't much better than the first. I should have taken art when I had the chance.

"Wait a minute," Mac said as we all sat in our church dining hall, eating pizza and subs. "How do we know the guy who is destined to open the gates again is the same one who opened them ten years ago?"

Glitch shrugged. "We don't, really. It's just a guess based on secondhand information."

"Yeah," I said after washing my pizza down with sweet tea. "That was the impression we got from the nephilim who came after me. They said he'd opened the gate once before, he'd do it again."

Mac nodded. "Okay, then my next question is, why hasn't he tried it again before now?"

"We wondered about that, too," Glitch said. "And we came to one conclusion."

"Which is?"

"We have no idea."

Brooklyn nodded, agreeing with Glitch's assessment.

"Well, okay, let's think about this."

"Got it," Glitch said, taking another bite of his favorite pizza: pepperoni with extra pepperoni. "Thinking now."

That boy cracked me up.

"There has to be a reason he hasn't tried again," Mac said, his gaze lowered in thought.

"Oh, I know!" Brooke said. "Maybe when Lor stabbed him with that stick, it got all infected and he almost died and has been in a coma for the last ten years."

"That's one theory," Granddad said. "You have another, Mac?"

Mac lifted one shoulder in a halfhearted shrug. "Maybe. I mean, unless he was out of the country . . . but even then, why couldn't he just open the gates somewhere else?"

"In that case," Grandma said, "if he were out of the country for some reason, then maybe location is important. Maybe he's limited. Can open the gates only in certain places."

Grandpa nodded. "Or it could even be a time issue. Maybe he can open the gates only during certain events."

"Like the planets aligning or something?" Glitch asked.

"Something exactly like that."

"There are so many possibilities," Mac said. "Perhaps whatever he used to open them, a grimoire of some kind—"

"A grimoire?" Kenya asked. She was eating a vegetable sub. Which seemed kind of pointless to me, but to each her own.

"It's like a textbook of magic. He may have gotten his hands on one, used it to open the gates, and when that went south, planned on trying again later, but something happened."

"What?"

"That's what I'd like to know. Sheriff?"

Sheriff Villanueva sat deep in thought as well.

"Is there any way to check hospital records on the day that the man was stabbed?"

"Not sure," he mumbled. "It's unlikely I could get anything concrete with the amount of time we have, but I could try. A stab wound isn't all that common."

"What about arrest records?" Mac asked.

"You think he's been in prison?"

Mac nodded. "Why else would it take him this long to organize a second attempt? He wanted what's inside Lorelei. He didn't get it. Why would it take him this long to try again?"

"He did want it," I said. "He summoned Malak-Tuke specifically. Only one demon came through the portal he'd opened. Hundreds of spirits, but only one demon." I held up an index finger to emphasize my point.

"He had to have thought he could control it somehow," Mac said. "I mean, demon possessions don't typically end well."

Cameron licked his fingers loudly, then said, "Lorelei is

the only one we've ever heard of like this. Most don't live longer than a month or two."

"Exactly, but that's because of who Lorelei is. He chose to be inside her. If Malak-Tuke had possessed Dyson, Dyson would surely have had a way to control him without it killing him first."

"If he did have a grimoire," Jared said, "maybe he had a means of controlling it once it got inside him."

A wave of unrest rippled within me. I wrapped an arm around my stomach even though it wasn't centrally located. It was everywhere. In all my cells at once.

Jared leaned over and whispered to me. "Are you okay?" He smelled clean, like rain in the forest.

"Yeah, I think Malak knows we're talking about him. And I don't think he likes the idea of being controlled."

"Who does?"

"Pix," Mac said, seeming hesitant about what he was about to say. "Can you communicate with it?"

I lowered my head. "I'm sorry. I can't. I mean, right after he entered me I felt him. It was like we thought the same thoughts, the same feelings. We were one. But I lost that a long time ago. He just kind of disappeared. Became a part of me."

"Are you sure you can't talk to it?"

I let a hapless smile through. "No. I'm not sure about anything."

"For a long time after the incident," Grandma said, "she never used the word 'I' anymore. She said 'we.' We want this or we want that."

"And let me guess," he said, fixing a knowing gaze on me. "They looked at you worriedly. So much so, that you eventually repressed that side of you, that part."

"I don't know. Maybe." Truth was, I hardly remembered

that time of my life. I just remembered the emptiness of losing both my parents in one shot and knowing it was my fault. I'd led them to their deaths. Pointed the way. I could hardly look in a mirror for months afterwards.

"Do you think you could try?" Mac asked.

"Sure. I can try."

Maybe because the end of the world was nigh or maybe because their parents didn't like me anymore, but that night Brooklyn and Glitch were ordered to go to their respective homes. Brooke's mom took her out of school, so she wouldn't be going tomorrow. Both sets of parents were members of the Order. They believed. They knew what was coming. Neither had qualms about their children helping us, but they did want to spend some time with their kids. Just in case.

I could understand that.

Kenya, Mac, and my grandparents as well as several other members of the Order were still up, chatting downstairs. Though they invited me to stay with them, I chose to go to my room. I sat alone, but I knew my ever-diligent bodyguards were hard at work below. Cameron was probably camped out in his truck. His dad had brought him takeout and a blanket, so he would probably be there all night.

And Jared would be on guard from his apartment. He'd had to run out for a little while that afternoon and see to another possession. Each time, he gave the spirit a chance to leave the human willingly. They never chose to do that. They'd possessed their prey on purpose, for that very reason. So that Jared would have no choice but to extract them, to end their existence in this realm and all others. They would simply cease to be.

Sheriff Villanueva wasn't having any luck with prison records that fit our time frame or with hospital records of men with stab wounds. He was widening his search, but we just didn't have that much time left. I didn't hold out much hope, but I knew I'd recognize him if I saw him again. In fact, I had seen him. A lot. I just couldn't place where. It was the same feeling as having a name stuck on the tip of my tongue. It was right there. So, so close.

And I had one day to remember. One day before Dyson opened the gates and the earth was flooded with thousands, possibly millions of dark spirits and demons. The thought crushed me. I felt like I should be doing something to prepare, but what?

I took the journal my dad found off my nightstand. I'd already looked at the drawings in it a hundred times, but could I go into them? Could I get anything from them? Why would my grandmother Olivia swipe this from the nephilim who took her? Why would she risk her life for it? What significance did it hold?

I decided to give it a shot. I scooted down so that my head was nowhere near my headboard. A concussion now would not help our cause. After settling in and preparing myself mentally, I concentrated. Gradually, like someone pressed slow motion, I entered the picture, only this time I didn't go into a scene. The drawing of the picture was the scene. I literally watched as the image I'd chosen was being drawn, but it was wrong. The world was wrong. Out of focus.

I held the pencil with my left hand. I tried to examine that hand, to look for a clue, but I reached over for a glass first and took a long draw of a fiery liquid. Whiskey. It was smooth and felt good when it hit my stomach. The prophet was coming. I'd seen the signs, and she was actually coming. The only one who could stop him, according to the grimoire, was on her way.

I'd have to make sure she got my message, but how? If I only knew who she was. If I only had those kinds of connections, but the Order of Sanctity was a tight-knit bunch. They weren't telling me anything. Idiots. I was only trying to help. I would give it to one of the members and hope it eventually ended up in the girl's hands. She could decipher it. Only her.

After slamming the snifter down, I went back to the drawing. I didn't have much time. He was beginning to suspect. But the drawing tilted. No, everything tilted until I could hardly work. I'd drunk too much that evening, and my drawing was not coming out as planned. I decided to give it a try anyway.

I lifted the journal, perched it on its side, and flipped through the pages, slowly at first, then again only faster. The images blurred together, blended to form the message, and I smiled. Right up to the minute my stomach lurched and I threw up over the side of my desk.

I rocketed back to reality, my head thrown back, my legs kicking out, my muscles straining to break free, but at least this time I seemed to have a little more control. Or so I thought until I, too, heaved, and the contents of my stomach raced up the back of my throat. I barely had time to pitch my torso over the side of the bed and empty my stomach onto a throw rug.

It was not pleasant.

I fell back onto my bed afterwards, swearing never to drink whiskey again as long as I lived. In a valiant effort, I gathered my strength and rolled off the bed. After tossing the rug onto the fire escape, I hurried to my bathroom and brushed my teeth. I could still taste the whiskey, could still feel it coursing through my veins.

But I hadn't really drank it. I tried to remind myself of that when I staggered back to my bed, woozy and weak, and took the journal again. Then I copied the man in the vision. I turned it onto its side and flipped through the pages. It was like watching a movie backwards. I did it wrong. Holding the book high in the air, I turned it over and fanned the pages again. A picture materialized. It was dark. Blurry.

What looked like a simple line in one image became part of a bigger picture when blended together with other lines from another page. What looked like a simple box formed a house of some kind. No, a building. Other lines became a van. Curves became a face at the end, as though someone were looking into a camera. And then it stopped as abruptly as it started. That was it? A van? A face? What on earth?

In the back of the book was what looked like a compass, but underneath was a map. I realized it was a map of New Mexico. Four towns were circled forming north, south, east, and west. Lines from each, one horizontal and one vertical, formed a crosshair. And right in the middle was the Abo Canyon, where the mission ruins were located. Where Dyson originally opened the gates of hell.

Someone was trying to warn us, but who? And what exactly was he trying to say?

I tried the journal one more time in an attempt to figure out that very thing. If it was about the gates, we were finding his message far too late. It had already happened. I breathed deep and concentrated on the book. The fanning pages lasted only a couple of seconds, like a really short movie. I flipped through them again, this time concentrating on the van. It had lettering, but I'd barely caught a glimpse before the movie ended. So I tried again. Each time I would see a little bit more, another piece of the puzzle would fall into place, until I could make out the lettering on the van. The eyes on the face, and I couldn't help but notice those were the same eyes I'd drawn that very day. They were Dyson's, but the van read SYDOW ELECTRIC.

I rushed downstairs. Ms. Mullins was there, sitting at the kitchen table with my grandparents, Betty Jo, and a couple of the church elders. Kenya had been napping on the sofa in our living room. She stirred when I yelled across the room.

"I figured out the journal!" I said, excited beyond measure. I hurried to the computer Grandma had set up as her little kitchen office, sat down, and typed in "Sydow Electric."

Everyone gathered around me, even a sleepy Kenya, but the sheriff became especially interested.

"Where did you get that name from?"

"The journal. It's a movie. It's like a really short animated movie. But it's a message to us. The guy was drunk, though, so I can only attest to one thing. I am never drinking whiskey."

"Pix," Grandma said, kneeling behind me. "What are you talking about?"

Kenya rubbed her eyes. "I fell asleep, sorry."

"It's okay. You'll be punished later," I said, trying to figure out why she was apologizing.

Jared came in then, soaked to the bone. He flashed a grin as rain dripped off his hair and down his face. Wet looked so good on him.

"It's raining?" I asked, and everyone gawked at me.

"Didn't you hear the thunder?" Mac asked.

"Oh, no, but I've been busy." When Jared winked at me, I repeated my earlier statement. "I figured out the journal!"

Then I went back to my search as they took turns with the journal, trying to see the movie.

I paused and took it from them. "Like this," I said, showing them how to do it.

Granddad tried next but soon pressed his mouth together in disappointment. One by one, everyone tried it, but no one, not even Jared, could see the movie. Weird. I saw it clearly now.

"That's it!" I nearly squeaked as an image popped up on screen. The exact same image from the journal. "That's in the movie!"

It was a photograph of a business located in . . . Riley's Switch, New Mexico. I stilled.

"It's here," I said. "The business is here."

"I remember it," the sheriff said.

Granddad nodded. "I do, too. Sydow was an odd sort, but a good man."

"Okay," Ms. Mullins said, taking a chair and sitting beside me. "This is an obituary. The man who owned this business died in '92." She scrolled down, mumbling to herself as she read. "Here we go. He is survived by two sons, Brian and Norman."

"Brian," I said, thinking back. "My name was Brian."

"Pix," Mac said, "you're going to have to help us out here. How was your name Brian?"

Another picture scrolled past, and I told Ms. Mullins to stop. "That's the man. That's him."

"Sweetheart," she said, her voice soft, "this man died twenty years ago. It can't be him."

My hope rushed out of me. "But he has the same eyes."

"Okay," Granddad said, "what did you mean, your name was Brian?"

"My name. No." I rubbed my forehead to clear the cobwebs. I was being silly and possibly still a little drunk. "The man's name, the one who drew that journal, was Brian. He was trying to send us a message. He said he didn't have much time."

Ms. Mullins did another search. "Brian Sydow. Okay, there was a Brian Sydow from Albuquerque, but he died twelve years ago as well."

She showed me the picture on the screen. "That's him. I can feel it. Does it say how he died?"

"No, just that he's survived by one brother, Norman Sydow."

"Okay, let's search him."

After a few minutes and a couple of cold trails, we finally came across a Norman Sydow in Ohio.

"There's no picture," Ms. Mullins said.

"There's always a picture. Somewhere, somehow, there will be—"

Before the picture even popped up, I'd figured it out. After rolling my eyes, I took a pen and paper, wrote out Norman's name, and then circled the "No" and the "Syd." "Okay, if you read that backwards, what do you have?"

"Dyson," Mac said. "It's him."

"Pretty smart," Jared said.

I lifted a shoulder bashfully. "Thanks. I've had a rather large amount of whiskey tonight. I think it helped." Grandma's jaw fell open and I laughed. "Just kidding, although I did throw up on my throw rug. Get it?" I snorted. "Throw up? Throw rug? It's on the fire escape."

Sheriff Villanueva had been taking notes the whole time. He shut his little black book and said, "Okay, I'm going back to the office to run this name."

"That's him."

Ms. Mullins had pulled up another link. It had an article about the arrest of an Ohio man on assault charges. "According to this article, Norman Sydow was sentenced to fifteen years in the Ohio State Pen for assaulting an officer and causing great bodily harm."

"Which would explain why he hasn't tried to open the gates in ten years."

"But that's him," I said, astonished. "That's the man who opened the gates in the first place."

Mac kneeled beside me. "Are you sure, Pix?"

I couldn't believe that after all this time, he was standing there, staring me in the face. The mug shot of him was horrible quality, but it was enough for recognition to spike inside me. It was him. "I'm positive," I said, unable to take my eyes off the screen.

"Good enough for me," he said.

"And I remember where I've seen him," I continued. "His dad was an electrician?"

"Yes," Ms. Mullins said. "Is that how you know him?"

My recognition stunned me. "He was a maintenance man at Bedford Fields."

"What?" the sheriff said, taking down that information as well.

"He was working there. How did I not recognize him?"

Mac tugged a curl. "It doesn't matter, Pix. We have him now."

"We did it." Grandma stared straight ahead in astonishment. "No." She turned to me. "You did it."

I tore my gaze away. After all this time, it couldn't be that simple. And he could've killed me at any time. Why didn't he? I looked over at Kenya. Was she really protecting me that much? Was it fate? I had so many questions, but we had bigger fish to fry. My questions would have to wait.

"You did it," Grandma repeated.

"Well, me and the whiskey."

I really had to stop teasing her about the whiskey. She went from proud to lethal on a dime, she was that good.

"And Brian," I continued. "Brian Sydow didn't have much time when he made this journal. I got the feeling he was sick and, obviously, dying. He was trying to get the journal into the hands of one of the members of the Order. He said I'd know what to do with it."

"And you did," Mac said. "He must have found Olivia and given it to her."

"She didn't get it from the nephlim," Granddad said. "She got it from Brian, whose brother, he knew, was going to open the gates of hell."

"Okay, I'll let you know what I find," the sheriff said as he tore out the door and into the rain.

I looked up. "I can't believe it's raining."

"That's it," Jared said. He took my hand and lifted me out of the chair. "No more whiskey for you."

"Oh, trust me. That is never going to happen again as long as I live."

"Bill." Grandma glared at my very innocent grandfather, her expression murderous. "Where did our granddaughter get whiskey?"

"What? Why are you looking at me?"

I giggled as Jared helped me upstairs. Mac stood, went to the door, and yelled out for Cameron to get up there and chaperone. He was at the window before we'd finished climbing the stairs. Man, that guy was fast. Darn it.

"I'm getting pretty good at that stuff," I said when Jared

led me to my door. I kept my hand on his arm as though to steady myself.

"Yes, you are." A sly grin lifted one corner of his mouth. "And you still won't get anything."

"Crap." I removed my hand and crossed my arms over my chest. "I have other ways, mister. Just you wait."

He lowered his head, his eyes sparkling underneath his boyishly long lashes. "I am well aware of that." Then he glanced at me from underneath all that length. "I've known for centuries."

BOLO

The next day Mr. Davis, the principal of Riley High, came over. We'd had a lot of that. Of people coming over. Bringing food. Hanging out and waiting for the world to end together. Not everyone knew what role I was supposed to play in all this, so their glances were not expectant, not hopeful like the glances of those who did know. I liked the clueless glances better.

Mr. Davis asked to speak to Jared alone, and my curiosity almost got the better of me when they excused themselves to our living room, where they closed the pocket door. Thunder rolled across the sky as the sheriff came in. We looked up from breakfast and stared at him, hoping he had good news.

"According to the Ohio State Penitentiary, Sydow was released six months ago and hasn't been seen since."

"What?" Brooke said. I'd filled both her and Glitch in the second they and their parents arrived, especially the part about how we should steer clear of whiskey at all costs. "Isn't he on parole or something?"

"Yes, he's supposed to be. But he never checked in with his parole officer. He's currently listed as a fugitive from the law."

"Which means what?" Granddad asked.

"It means nobody has the slightest idea where he is."

"I bet I could take a guess," Cameron said. He'd come in from the rain for a plate of bacon, eggs, and fried potatoes.

"But we know who he is," I said, pleading with them. "What he looks like. We can stop him, right?"

"I'm working on it, hon. It'll take some time, but I have a BOLO out on him. If he's anywhere in this county, we'll find him."

Not long after the sheriff left, Jared came out of the living room with a very pale Mr. Davis. He said his good-byes and left through the store out the front door. I asked Jared, "Did you tell him who you are?"

He shrugged as he piled a plate high. "I didn't see the point in not telling him," he said.

Brooklyn pointed her fork at him. "So, he knows you took his brother?"

"He knows."

"And he's okay with that?"

"I'm not sure," he said, stabbing a potato and lifting it to his mouth. "Once I told him I could kill an entire army with a single touch, he didn't ask many questions."

The storm churned above us all morning, the rain hard and unforgiving. Granddad and Mac went out in search of any place Dyson might hide while the sheriff checked all the hotels and rental properties. Today was literally our last day on earth if we didn't get this figured out soon. If we didn't find Dyson soon.

But the clouds were beginning to worry me. They looked an awful lot like my vision. Low. Dark. Volatile.

Brooke hung up her phone. We were hanging in my bedroom, watching gag reels from our favorite movies on the Internet when her mom called. "Okay," she said, "Mom said for us to meet everyone at the church. That's going to be our headquarters, so we're supposed to bring—"

"What day is it?" I asked, gazing out into the storm, a little mesmerized.

"Saturday."

Jared was also gazing out into the storm, and Cameron was literally out in it, standing on the fire escape.

I stepped to Jared, my heart breaking into a million pieces. "It's today, isn't it?"

He offered only the barest hint of a nod, seeming as surprised as I was. Cameron opened the window and climbed in, soaking my floor. He shook off some of the water, then regarded us with a grim expression.

"We doing this or not?"

Jared nodded again. "We're doing it."

Brooke stood slowly while Glitch and Kenya looked on. "I thought we had another day."

And that, too, would be my fault. "I'm sorry. I got my days mixed up."

"No," Cameron said. "If you included the day you saw everything, if you included Tuesday, then that would be five days. From what I understand, visions aren't an exact science."

Brooke stood cemented to the spot. "We have to call everyone. We have to warn them."

The look Cameron gave her was so full of longing, so full of what-ifs, I wanted to cry. "I've failed," I said, stunned. I was actually beginning to believe all the crap flying around. All the prophecies and promises that I was magically going to figure it out. But those were not normal clouds. The gates were opening, and they were opening fast.

I grabbed my jacket. "He has to be out there," I said, readying to leave. "He has to be out in this. It's the only way."

Jared and Cameron exchanged charged looks. "We'll find him," Jared said.

"I'm going with you."

"No, Lorelei, I can't let you do that."

"Let me rephrase that," I said, stepping close. "I'm not leaving you. And I'm not letting you leave me. If this is all the time we have left, we're spending it together."

Before he could reply, Cameron questioned Brooke with his eyes, his expression fierce. "Brooke?" he asked.

"I wouldn't dream of missing this."

"I'm in," Glitch said, grabbing his jacket as well.

"Oh, hell yes," Kenya said, and I decided to write her enthusiasm off as naïveté.

We piled into Cameron's truck, but Kenya said she forgot something and ran back inside. She climbed in the bed, which thankfully had a camper shell, and we tore out of the parking lot with a vengeance. Brooke called her parents to tell them what was going on, and I tried to call my grandparents, but no one picked up. Really? At a time like this? They really were the worst with their phones.

Brooke's mom promised to let them know; then she begged Brooke to get to the church. "I will, Mom, as soon as we get this taken care of."

I squeezed my eyes shut, praying for strength, for guidance, and for superpowers.

Just like in my visions, the clouds churned with an eerie darkness that reminded me of a cauldron from a witch's brew. Fear didn't consume me. It was there, but it didn't consume me. Regret consumed me. The realization that we had failed consumed me. The war was starting and I didn't stop it. The prophecies—the dozens of prophecies that promised their believers deliverance from this horror by means of a powerful descendant of Arabeth—were wrong. Plain and simple. Or they simply put their money on the wrong girl.

I wasn't strong enough. Or perhaps I wasn't smart enough. Whatever it was I was supposed to do to stop the war before it ever started did not come about. I'd messed up somewhere. I'd taken a wrong turn. And because of it, the world was going to pay a very high price.

Tears stung my eyes from both the emotion roiling inside me and the wind whipping my hair across my face. We found the center of the storm and assumed Dyson would be there, so that's where we got out. Cameron and Jared took swords out of the bed of the truck. They'd clearly been prepared for my failure, not a good feeling.

A particularly strong gust of rain and wind almost brought

me to my knees. I caught myself and looked up. In the middle of the cauldron, a vortex spun and swirled.

"Look!" I cried above the noise.

Everyone watched as its center opened and dark, inklike beings, fleshless shadows in the air, slithered out. Each one paused, seemed to get its bearings, then darted off in whichever direction it chose. Some headed toward Riley's Switch. Some scurried over the landscape toward bigger and better seas. Albuquerque. Santa Fe. Las Cruces. And beyond. They would soon spread through the sky like a monumental murder of crows, attacking people as they went.

It was exactly as I'd envisioned it. I stood watching the horror unfold before my eyes. Kenya stood beside me, ever faithful, ever naïve.

I yelled to her above the stinging rain. "It's over!" I said, my voice barely audible. "I've failed."

But Kenya was in shock. Eyes wide, mouth hanging open, she'd never imagined what it would look like. She'd never imagined it would come to this, her faith so complete. She'd brought me something. In her hand was a stack of old photographs, growing wetter by the second.

That's what she'd gone back for? Pictures?

I looked away from her, sorrow eating me from the inside out. I'd let her down so monumentally. So completely.

We watched as Jared went in search of Dyson. Cameron stayed close, shielding his eyes from the rain, waiting for a signal from Jared. But none came. Jared disappeared over the landscape, the grayness of the day making it impossible to follow him for long.

The shadows were getting closer. Anytime they got too close, Cameron would move to block them, but their numbers were growing by the second. We couldn't do this all day.

Just then we spotted Jared jogging back to us. He motioned for us to get in the truck. They were following him, a group of the shadows, and he transformed before our eyes. He'd become something other. He'd become like them, and I stood transfixed as I watched him. Mesmerized. One moment he was as solid as I was. Broad shoulders. Solid stance. Muscles straining against the weight of the sword he wielded. The next, he was smoke. A magnificent phantom fighting ghosts, the spirits of those sent to hell. They'd been sent for a reason and they fought dirty. They came at him in droves. Nipped at him. Ripped at his smoky essence until pieces of him came off in what I could only assume was their mouths.

He faltered and they pounced like hungry jackals. My hands flew to my mouth as he disappeared beneath them.

I tried to run to him, but Cameron pushed me back. I stumbled, fell to the ground, looked up at him with a new anger bursting inside me, and screamed. "What is the use?" I yelled above the roar of the wind, freezing rain pelting my face like frozen razor blades.

Brooklyn huddled beside me, shaking from the cold. "What does it matter now?"

Cameron turned on me, his anger matching my own. "If you don't do this soon, there will be nothing left to save!"

Was he kidding me? Do what? I decided to ask him as another spirit rushed forward only to be thwarted by him, a nephilim. For some reason, they didn't seem to be able to enter him. But I had no idea what he wanted me to do.

"Do what?" I screamed again. "Do what, do what, do what, do what?"

He bent down to me, lifted me to my feet by my saturated shirt collar, and growled in my face, "Do what it is that you do, and do it fast. You are the only one who can stop this."

Glitch stood in shock. I followed his gaze to Kenya. She was on the ground, her head thrown back, her spine arched to the point of snapping. Her eyes had rolled into her head until only the white remained. The horrific scene was a re-play of what I'd already seen. Soon her bones would break, one by one, just like in my vision.

I ran and threw myself over her in an attempt to stop the spasms. Brooklyn did the same. She followed me, fell to her knees, tried to stop Kenya's head from thrashing. Realizing somewhere deep inside how ridiculous my actions were, I screamed above the wind for whatever was inside her to stop. It did not hear me. Or it chose not to listen.

Kenya started convulsing. The tendons in her neck stretched to near breaking point; her arms, locked and rigid, did the same. Her spasming legs lifted her off the ground, arched her back until, to my complete and utter horror, her spine snapped. Before I could try to pull her to me, to cradle her, Cameron appeared. Without hesitation, he took her head into his hands and twisted. She died instantly, collaps-ing into my arms. Brooklyn pressed one hand to her mouth. She swayed as though about to pass out.

After a moment, Kenya released the pictures she'd brought. They fluttered out of her hands and spread in the wind, curl-ing and flipping like fall leaves. I buried my face in the crook of her neck and Brooklyn did the same to me. She took hold of my hand, squeezing and crying and praying.

I saw sneakers standing beside me. I looked up at Glitch. He blinked, his gaze moving away from the horrific scene before him, watching the photographs dance around us. He reached up. Tried to catch one. Missed. Then, as if it were the only thing that mattered—that one photograph that was of no importance whatsoever—he sprinted after it. He dodged past plundering spirits, updrafts of rain and wind, and sagebrush.

The rain was becoming colder and colder. The wind stronger and stronger. It literally dragged me off Kenya, out of Brooklyn's embrace as though it had an agenda. We clutched on to each other and watched as Glitch dived through the air for the picture. With all the dirt and rain swirling around him, I couldn't tell if he caught it or not. He fell to the earth on his stomach and slid a good five feet in the muddy, unforgiving terrain of the New Mexico desert.

Then the thing I feared most happened. A thundering crash sounded close by, like something falling to the earth. A thick, black smoke gathered and centralized until it started forming mass, taking shape. Soon wide shoulders topped the trees just beyond the clearing. An animalistic head. A demon materialized before us.

That was when I caught sight of Jared again. He had escaped the melee. I had no idea how, but a joy that I thought I'd never feel again spread through me. He sought me out, gave me a quick once-over, then scrambled past the other spirits itching for a piece of him, and slid until he stood before the demon, sword at the ready. But another thundering crash sounded beside that one. A puff of mud and water rose up like a meteor had crash-landed; then another demon materialized beside the first one. Then another.

Three demons, each the size of a three-story building, stood before him.

I'd seen him fight one before. I'd had a vision of that very thing before I ever met him. He'd fought hard, been wounded, but eventually he prevailed. It was not an easy victory, and that was against just one. There were three. And probably more on the way.

I stood up, fighting the wind with every ounce of strength I had. Jared could not fight them alone, and Cameron wouldn't leave my side. I had no choice but to release the beast inside me. I didn't know how to summon him exactly, so I just thought about it really hard and ordered him out. I needed him. He'd been crashing at my place, literally, for a decade. It was time he earned his rent.

An acidic smoke exited out of my lungs and started to take shape beside me. It burned my throat and left me even colder than I already was. When Malak-Tuke formed fully, I pointed to where Jared fought.

"Help him," I said, and Malak was gone.

The demons were so fast. So lethal. Solid muscle complemented with speed and a thirst for blood. But Malak took them by surprise. They hadn't expected a fight with one of their own. The first one met its demise with a handful of claws across the throat, almost beheaded in one lethal swipe. The second readied himself, prepared to square off against the great Malak-Tuke.

Jared fought the third—a scene that reminded me of David and Goliath—as Malak brought the other one down, but only for a moment. Their movements were so fast, my eyes could hardly keep up. They were struggling upright one moment, then wrestling on the ground the next.

I heard another thunderous crash in the distance and knew that another demon had entered this plane. Dyson had to be close. He just had to be. If I could stop him, we might could figure out a way to close the gates. He would have the book, the grimoire, if there was such a thing. We could use it. We could stop it.

Malak disentangled himself from the other demon and straightened to his full height. Though he looked exactly like the other three, I knew he was the victor, because I knew him. Had for a long time. He'd been living inside me, and we now thought very much alike, so when I said to him, "Get Dyson!" I knew he'd know what to do.

He turned and looked across the land from his imperial vantage point. Then he took off. A mass of flesh and fog, muscle and sinew, he sped over the land and through the trees until he disappeared. I called after him, "And bring me the book!"

I didn't get a reply. Malak wasn't the talkative type, but I was certain he would hear me.

Jared had almost downed the third demon. It fell to one giant knee, and he brought his sword at the ready, a fine sheen of sweat on his skin glimmering in what little light filtered through the storm.

Another thunderous crash sounded in the distance. That made five. Two down. One on the way out. Two left. How many more would come through before we could get the gate closed?

"Lorelei!"

I turned to see Glitch trying to get back to me. He was waving his hand about, trying to show me something.

"I got one!"

One? A picture? Had he caught one of the pictures Kenya brought out? Why? I thought, as despair so deep and desperate tried to get a foothold on my emotions. I'd lost sight of Brooke and could no longer see Kenya's body.

I turned back to Glitch. A tree behind him started to wobble. Not just bend to the wind's will, but wobble as though it were going to topple over. As Glitch struggled to get to me, it tipped sideways and I realized it would fall right in his path. I screamed to him and pointed, but he didn't see me through the maelstrom. He ran, holding the photograph above his head as the tree descended far faster than I thought possible. As though it were aiming for him. Targeting him.

I pointed again and again, screaming louder and louder. The second I thought to summon Malak—surely he could stop it, surely he could get here in time—the tree crashed to the ground. Even more dirt and debris rose until visibility was all but gone. I lost sight of Glitch completely.

Though I could see almost nothing, I ran forward, stumbling over the uneven ground. I heard Cameron call my name, then Brooklyn, but I couldn't see them either. Their voices grew distant, but I continued forward until a branch stabbed my shoulder.

I'd found the tree, and I called out to Glitch. Again and again as I searched blindly through sharp, protruding limbs. They scratched and scraped as I fought them. I fell to my hands and knees and crawled until my hands found something soft and warm. I held back the attacking branches and looked down. It was the back of Glitch's head.

"Glitch!" I scurried around, angling for a better look, then regretted it.

His eyes were open, his stare blank, lifeless. Fresh blood flowed from a wound on his head, down until it dripped onto his eyelashes, over the bridge of his nose, and across his cheek.

I gaped in disbelief. It wasn't real. None of this was real.

The wind seemed to be dying down and I caught sight of Brooklyn. She'd tried to follow me and lay barely fifteen feet away. Lay. I watched, waiting for her to move. Her head rested on an arm. It was the exact same position she slept in.

One arm below her head, her hand hanging over the side of the bed. I waited for her to wake as I'd done so many times before, but she didn't move. The entire time I looked on, she didn't move.

Then I saw Cameron rush to her. He slid to a stop beside her, lifted her into his arms. Her limp body looked like a rag doll as he wrapped his arms around her. Brushed her hair out of her face.

I turned and watched as one demon fell to Jared's sword and another appeared. Jared had turned to search for me, and in a lightning quick move, the demon raked his claws across Jared's back. He stumbled to his knees, fought for balance, and brought his sword up again. That was when I realized he was covered in blood. The rain was washing it off almost as fast as it flowed out of him. Another gust blocked my sight of him just as he prepared to attack.

Farther south, Malak reappeared. He was fighting two more demons. The earth rumbled with another thunderous crash, but it wasn't the fall of one of the demons. It was the fall of Malak. They'd downed him, this beast who'd switched sides. Who'd tried to protect me.

I looked at Glitch's hand beside me. It held the picture he'd been trying so desperately to get to me. I took it from his grasp but couldn't make it out through the blur of tears and rain. The colors were running anyway, so I had no clue what the picture had captured. Why would a photograph be so damned important that he risked his life to get it? That he gave his life trying to get it back to me?

My muscles were seizing, and I realized I was sobbing outright. This wasn't real. Things like this didn't happen. Not really. I crumpled the picture, closed my eyes, and crumbled to the dirt.

"Lorelei."

I heard my name, but it was soft, melodic, unhurried.

"You're going to be late."

Late? What on earth could be so important that I had to worry about being late during the apocalypse? Shouldn't all appointments be canceled in times of earth's total devastation? During the annihilation of humanity?

I couldn't bring myself to open my eyes again. Ever. I couldn't see the lifeless bodies of my best friends. The image was already branded in my mind, cauterized in my brain. Just let me die, I thought over and over. Just take me now.

"I'd hate to be you if you're late for Ms. Mullins's class one more time. She threatened to hang you by your toes the last time."

I felt a softness, a warmth, being dragged off me. As though I were covered in a blanket. Then my feet were being tickled. My legs jerked in response.

"I knew that'd work," a male voice said. One I didn't recognize.

"We have a big day ahead of us. It's *your* day, remember? You've been harping about this day since you were six." The world around me shook as though I were on a trampoline and someone was bouncing beside me. "You can have anything you want for breakfast, so you'd best be deciding. This is a limited-time offer."

I pried my eyes open, squinting against the barrage of rain and debris that would soon assault them until I realized the wind had died down. Completely. I didn't even hear a soft breeze. My hair didn't fly about my face nor did my skin sting with droplets of ice. I relaxed my lids and let them slide open farther. But I saw nothing. Just white. White all around me. White and bright and airy.

Someone brushed a lock of hair off my face. A man. A man was sitting beside me. Adrenaline shot through me as I screeched and scrambled off the bed.

The bed.

I'd been on a bed.

My brows snapped together as I tried to gain my bearings. Where was the tree? Where were Glitch and Brooklyn and Cameron and Jared?

The man stood, startled by my reaction, then kneeled on the other side of the large bed, his expression soft, knowing. "You were having a bad dream," he said, offering me a sympathetic smile. "It's okay. None of it was real."

I tried to focus on his words, but I couldn't quite get past the part that he looked alarmingly like my dad. I stared at him in awe as he placed his chin on the mattress and gave me a moment to recover.

"You okay, Pix?" he asked.

Then I felt a hand on my shoulder. I shrank back, cowering in the corner.

"Heavens, sweetheart," a woman said. "That must have been a bad one. But today's the big day. Maybe—" She looked across the mattress at the man, her expression full of sorrow. "—maybe it'll be better after today, just like you said."

This woman, with her gentle smile and her large blue eyes, looked so much like my mother, my chest tightened around my heart.

And then it hit me. I'd died. Thank God, I'd died and gone to heaven to be with my parents. And I hadn't even felt any pain. This was wonderful.

But just to make sure, I said hesitantly, "Mom?"

She fixed a patient smile on me.

"Are you my mom?"

Once again, she glanced across the bed before returning her attention to me. "No," she said, her face turning sorrowful. "I'm your aunt Edna." Then she laughed softly. "Of course I'm your mom, silly. Do you want to talk about your dream?"

"And, and you're my dad?" I asked the man.

"Sorry, Pix," he said, shaking his head. "I'm your great-uncle Ferdinand. We haven't met yet, but I'm from Spain. I don't really know any English, so we'll have to learn sign language or something to communicate." When I frowned at him, he continued. "That was a really bad one, right?"

Everything hit me at once. My friends were gone. My grandparents were gone. Jared was gone. Had they gone to heaven like me? Would I see them all again? Jared once told me he didn't get to heaven much. Would he come visit?

Their loss crashed into me. Seized my lungs. I was here with my parents, something I'd wanted for so long, I could hardly remember a time when I didn't, and yet everyone I'd ever known, everything I'd ever known was gone.

I looked up at my mother with her beautiful smile and flung myself into her arms. I didn't know if it was okay to cry in heaven, but I was doing it. Sobs racked my body so hard, I couldn't catch my breath. I cried out loud as my mother rocked me in her arms. Dad had come around and pulled us both into his warm embrace, and still I cried. I cried for the loss of the most wonderful grandparents in existence. The most amazing friends, who stuck by me through everything, even a supernatural war. The most beautiful boy I'd ever met, who'd liked me—me!—and told me I was pretty and smart and talented.

I cried so hard, my throat hurt and my eyes burned. Dad went to get a washcloth. Mom held it to my head as he lifted me up and placed me back on the bed. A white bed with a white comforter that looked like clouds. This was definitely heaven.

"I'm sorry," I said to them between sobs. "I'll miss everyone so much."

"Who, Pix?" Dad asked me.

I focused on him. On his red hair and scruffy jaw. His dark gray eyes. He was so handsome and he looked exactly as I remembered him. As did my mother.

"Do you want to stay home from school today?" Mom asked.

"School?" I asked, rather horrified. "I still have to go to school?"

"According to the law," Dad said. "And if you don't, I honestly think Mr. Davis would enjoy nothing more than hunting you down and throwing you in detention. You remember the last time you and Tabitha skipped."

Tabitha? Tabitha Sind? Why on earth would I skip school in heaven with Tabitha Sind? And how the heck did she get through the pearly gates? Didn't they have some kind of checklist? A set of standards? Morals one had to meet before you could pass?

"I just didn't think . . . I'm just surprised there's school in heaven."

It was odd that Ms. Mullins would still be my teacher even here and Mr. Davis would still be the principal. Surely there were others more qualified for an authoritative position in a celestial institution of higher learning. Literally.

"I figured I wouldn't have to go to school anymore."

Dad laughed. "Nice try, Pixie Stick, but you're not getting off that easily. If you hurry, you can still make the first bell."

"Maybe we shouldn't push her," Mom said to him. "Her dreams have never been this bad."

Dad shrugged. "It's up to you, Pix. Do you feel up to going to school?"

With a reluctant shrug, I said, "I guess." May as well jump in with both feet.

After showering in a bathroom made of Tuscan tile and marble and dressing in a closet bigger than my old room, I went down a gorgeous set of wood stairs until I landed on a stunning terra-cotta floor with a huge skylight above it. It was the stuff of my dreams, this living in heaven. I figured it would have streets of gold and clouds of ionized silver, but this would definitely do.

Even with the fact that I was with my parents once more, I felt dizzy, unstable. I didn't quite trust this version of heaven. What if I really were only dreaming?

"Okay," my dad said to me, a beautiful smile lighting his face. "Since you never gave a preference, I made your favorite, chocolate pancakes."

I looked over at the chocolate pancakes and almost seized, my pleasure was so strong. I didn't have the heart to tell him I'd never had chocolate pancakes. Clearly I'd been missing out. I'd have to confront my grandmother about this.

"And," Mom said, "two percent milk." She poured me a glass of ice-cold 2 percent.

"Because God forbid we have whole milk," Dad said.

I didn't like whole milk? Okay, good to know.

"A girl's gotta watch her figure," he continued, teasing me.

I looked down. Same straight skinny figure I'd always had. No idea why I was watching it now, but I'd go along with it. I'd go along with anything as long as my parents were with me.

I couldn't stop staring at them. Could hardly take my eyes off Dad when he placed a brown pancake on my plate followed by a healthy—or unhealthy, depending on one's perspective—helping of syrup.

"Just so you know," Mom said, giving Dad a warning shake of her finger, "when she ends up in the nurse's office, passed out from a sugar crash, you are going to pick her up and explain to the nurse what happened."

I dug in, taking a huge bite and moaning aloud when the sweet flavors danced across my taste buds. This really was heaven, and it had chocolate. But I still didn't take my eyes off them. Was this what they would have been like had they lived? Or maybe these were simply my memories, ones I'd suppressed, rising to the surface before I died completely.

Morbid but worth consideration.

I watched them as they teased each other, Mom dancing around Dad's threat to pinch an inch when she said she weighed no more than she had ten years earlier. "I like weight on a girl," he said, chasing her around the kitchen, "now eat these pancakes or I'll tie you down and force-feed you."

Mom giggled. Giggled like a schoolgirl, and my heart soared.

I looked down, not wanting to worry them when tears came to my eyes again. I'd cried for a solid twenty minutes earlier. I couldn't start again now. They'd send me to the loony bin. The one with padded walls and crazy nurses who make you swallow pills, then check under your tongue to make sure you didn't stash it. I'd never stashed anything under my tongue, and I had no intentions of starting now.

"Pix?" Dad asked. He frowned at me. "You can't be sad for your party tonight. Everyone will wonder about you. You know, more than they already do."

"Lucas!" Mom said, scolding him with a look. "No one wonders about our daughter."

"Oh, right," he said, nodding as he cleaned up his cooking area. "They don't have to wonder. They already know she's a bit off kilter."

Mom took his spatula and beat him with it as he blocked her blows with a dish towel.

This was not from my memories. This was new. This was heaven.

HEAVEN AND OTHER ODDITIES

Our house sat about half a mile back from my grandparents' health food store, the Wild 'n Wonderful. It was a beautiful white two-story with lots of wood and glass and plants. I wanted to explore it, to search out every nook and cranny, but according to the parental units, I had to get to school.

I smiled. I'd always wanted to say parental units. By the time I'd learned that phrase, mine were gone and it didn't seem right to call them such after the fact. It wouldn't have the same impact. The same implication.

Dad drove me to school. He played the radio too loud and sang along to Creedence Clearwater Revival's "Bad Moon Rising." Despite his joy, it had an ominous feel to it. I shook it off and just tried to accept. To enjoy. This was what I'd dreamed of for ten years. Why question it? Why stir the pot?

"I would've made a great hippie," Dad said, a forlorn kind of longing in his voice. "If I'd been born just a few years earlier, but noooooo. My parents wanted to wait until they could afford a child. What kind of nonsense is that? I totally missed the flower power generation."

He rambled on and on like that all the way to school, which sadly was only a few blocks. I could listen to him forever. I was certain he wasn't always that cheerful—everybody had a bad day here and there—but this was heaven after all.

"So, we still on for tonight?"

"Tonight?" I asked.

"The party. The one you've talked about—"

"Oh, right, I forgot," I said. The party, whatever that meant. I'd checked the calendar. It wasn't my birthday, so I wasn't quite sure why we were having a party that I'd apparently been insisting upon since I was six. But again, if my parents were involved, I'd so be there.

Riley High looked exactly as it always had. It was a relatively new school, only a couple of years old, but it was exactly as I remembered it. I liked school about as much as I liked working in my grandparents' store. I was always ready and willing to put the work in, but at the same time, I could think of a thousand things I'd rather be doing.

Dad dropped me off up front, then waited as I walked through the front doors. The gesture was endearing. Was he worried I'd be abducted in so short a span? And in heaven? Did people get abducted in heaven?

I strode through the front doors and sampled the air. It smelled the same. It looked the same. Everything was the same. I just really thought heaven would look a lot different from Riley's Switch, New Mexico. If anything, I thought it would resemble Hawaii a little more.

But maybe this was *my* heaven. Did each of us have our own version of heaven? Admittedly, in my perfect world, heaven consisted of what I already had with a couple of parents thrown in for good measure. I'd wanted only them. Nothing more. Nothing less.

Brooklyn was walking toward me, a wide smile on her face, and my heart soared. She was here. We'd be in heaven together. I started to wave until I realized she wasn't smiling at me, but just past me.

Turning, I saw Ashlee and Sydnee Southern walk in. Brooke hurried to them, and they instantly formed a huddle, clearly sharing some juicy tidbit of information. I heard whispers of a new guy, a hot new guy that Brooke would not believe.

"Brooklyn?" I said.

She turned to me. "Oh, hi. What's up?"

She acted like she barely knew me. Like we hadn't been best friends since the third grade.

"Nothing, I just—I wanted to see how you were doing."

Ashlee and Sydnee offered me a congenial smile, waiting patiently for me to give them back their friend. *Their* friend.

"Oh." Brooklyn frowned, confused. "I'm okay, Lorelei. It is Lorelei, right?"

I blinked and fought the sting in the back of my eyes. "Yes. It's Lorelei."

"Hey, we have to get to Mr. Burke's class early to turn in our late papers," Ashlee said. Or possibly Sydnee. I had no idea, actually. I never could tell them apart. "Find us after third."

"Will do," Brooke said before turning back to me. She giggled. "They're always turning in homework late."

"Right." I pressed my mouth together, becoming confused and discombobulated. "I'll just get to class, then."

Just as I stepped past her, she touched my arm. "Are you okay, Lorelei?"

Lorelei. Not Lor. Not Squeegee like she'd called me in grade school, but Lorelei. "Yes. I'm fine."

I was trying to get away from her again when she said, "I'm sorry about that."

"About what?" I asked.

"About your name. I knew it was Lorelei. Or, well, I was pretty sure it was Lorelei. I didn't mean to . . . I mean, it's just that being the newish girl in school, I had to learn so many names at once, I kind of get confused." She laughed. "Who am I kidding, I get confused anyway. Being seminew is just a good excuse, you know what I mean?"

"New?" I asked. Weren't we both new? Wasn't pretty much everyone in school new? "What do you mean?"

"Now who's confused?" she said. "Let's walk to science together."

Okay, we still had first hour together, so that hadn't changed.

"You'd think after being here for two months, I'd at least know the names of all the kids in my classes."

I bowed my head. Maybe time was different here. Brooke had died before me. Maybe in heaven time, that few minutes was more like two months.

"I've lived here my whole life, and I think there's a couple I still don't know. Is that awful?"

She laughed and wrapped an arm in mine. I wanted to throw mine around her, but she might find that odd.

"I like you," she said. "I have to be honest, I kind of felt this instant connection to you when I started school, but that could be because we're the same height. Five-foot-short."

I wanted to laugh at her joke, but I spotted my archnemesis headed toward us, a frown on her face.

"Lorelei," Tabitha said, her brows drawn sharply, "I've been trying to call you all morning. What am I going to wear?"

"I'll leave you two alone," Brooklyn said. She stepped away before I could clutch on to her arm and beg her to save me.

"I don't understand," I said to Tabitha, more than a little shocked that she was talking to me as opposed to, say, humiliating me mercilessly in front of the entire school.

"Tonight," she replied, her tone one of utter frustration. "The big party. Holy cow, you've been harping about it since . . . forever. But I don't know what to wear."

She started back down the hall, winding around a group of skaters like I was supposed to follow. So I did.

"I mean, how formal are we talking? I know they're cooking outside on the grill, but will we be eating outside? I'm not really fond of bugs in my food."

Her voice faded away when I spotted Hector Salazar. Back when I was alive, Hector brought a gun to school and shot Cameron three times before Cameron could get to him and break his neck. He'd died badly, but they let him into heaven anyway? Clearly their review board was dropping the ball. I ogled him so long, Tabitha had to take my arm and steer me past a kid drinking from the water fountain.

"Are you listening to me?" she asked. "You're so weird today. I know it's your day and all, but really. You should have sympathy for the rest of us who have to muddle through life without—" She lifted her hands and added air quotes to her next statement. "—'superpowers.'"

I stopped. "What superpowers?" Tabitha had never known about my visions, and I liked it that way. How could she know now? Did everybody know? And why the heck was she talking to me?

"Your superpowers," she said. "Oh . . . my God. You're going to drive me crazy. Your powers." She waved her arms as though that would help me understand. "Your ability to accessorize in a single bound. Your talent for matching the right shirt with just the right shoes and then taking an old ugly scarf and turning it into the perfect complement to any ensemble. Wow. I don't know what you had for breakfast," she said, urging me forward, "but you need to back off the bagels. That many carbs is bound to be bad for the brain."

"Hey, Lorelei," a girl I didn't know said to me. Now, that made sense. I could see everyone knowing everyone in heaven. Yet I didn't know her. That blew that theory. "Did you study for the test?"

Test? There were tests in heaven? I deflated even more.

I sat in first hour, listening to the indelible Ms. Mullins and wondering about lots and lots of things. Wasn't this heaven? What other explanation could there be?

I wrote a note and passed it back to Brooklyn. I didn't look behind me, but she took it. Always a good sign. My note said simply, *Are we in heaven?*

A minute later, she swiped the note across my shoulder.

I took it as nonchalantly as I could and opened it from under my desk.

I don't understand. I always considered physical science more like hell, myself. LOL.

I rolled my eyes, feeling like I was in a world turned upside down. The second the bell rang, I grabbed my backpack.

"Lorelei," Ms. Mullins said as I headed out the door. I'd wanted to catch up to Brooklyn, but she darted out before I could get her attention.

I headed back to the tiny teacher.

"I wanted to thank you for the invitation to your party tonight," she said, and I wondered if everyone who was new got a party. Then again, everyone in this school was new. Unless that whole time theory was accurate. "I'd love to go," she added.

"Oh, great. I'll let my parents know."

I thought about it all morning. My time theory. Remarkably, Brooke and I still had the same classes together, but we didn't sit next to each other in any of them. Clearly, we were not best friends in this reality. Every cell in my body ached just thinking about it. But so many things were exactly the same.

The kids were pretty much the same. If I was in heaven—though that theory was losing its shine fast—everyone in my school was already dead. The war had truly destroyed humanity. Or, well, Riley's Switch.

It broke my heart to know I'd failed. Just like I said I would. Just like I'd feared.

I decided to eat at the snack bar at lunch. I wasn't really hungry, but I wasn't not hungry.

"Three fifty," Madison Espinosa said.

I needed money in heaven, too? I groaned and checked

my pockets, worried I wouldn't have anything in them. I pulled out two ones.

"Um," I said, looking at my soda, bag of chips, and pastry, "can I put that back?"

She rolled her eyes. If this was heaven, they weren't very nice. "Sure." She grabbed the soda can. "Two twenty-five."

I patted my pockets, humiliation burning within me.

"Lorelei!" Brooklyn said. I didn't have to turn to recognize her voice. "Here's your change."

The surprised expression on my face made her laugh. "She'll take the soda, too. I had her money, so you can stop rolling your eyes at her."

"What's going on?" Tabitha said behind me.

"We have to talk," Brooklyn said to her. "If you don't mind my joining you."

Tabitha seemed at a loss, and it made me wonder where all her other friends were. Amber and Ashlee and Sydnee. Those were her crowd. Not me. Never me.

"I'm going home for lunch. I just thought Lor was going to join me, so I came to find her. But we can go alone. That's okay."

"We?" I asked her.

"Amber and me. Duh. Oh, and she wants to know what to wear, too."

How, alternate reality or not, did I ever get the ability to accessorize? I could barely find a matching sock every morning.

"Um, we'll have to go through her closet later."

"Like you don't know it backwards and forwards. But okay. After school, then. Don't forget. You know how she gets."

Tabitha bounced off as Brooklyn pointed to a table. Our table. The same one we'd been sitting at for two years.

"Is this okay?" she asked, putting her tray down.

"Sure. And, thanks. I forgot to get more money this morning," I said, lying through my teeth. I'd figured I didn't need any.

"No prob. Happens to me all the time."

We sat down, and in stellar Brooke fashion, she leveled a pointed stare on me. "Okay, spill."

"Spill?" I asked, opening my bag of chips.

"That note this morning. What was that about? You seemed . . . distressed."

I took a chip and crunched a moment before answering. "It's weird. I'm not sure how to explain it, and it's silly anyway."

"Weird, huh?" She put mustard on her burger and fries.

That was one of our favorite things to do, and we'd discovered it together. The joys of dipping fries in mustard instead of ketchup. But that was years ago, and if my newest calculations were right, we weren't actually in heaven. I had no idea where we were, but it wasn't heaven in the traditional sense. So if she didn't discover the magic mustard trick with me, then who?

"This whole day has been weird."

"Because you're weird," a boy behind me said.

I turned to see Glitch walk up. I'd yet to see him all day, and here he was in all his glory. I jumped up and threw my arms around him.

He stumbled back, but not because of me. I'd shocked him. I pulled away instantly, then stuttered, trying to explain my abrupt actions.

"I haven't seen you in a while," I said, flustered beyond belief when he just stared at me aghast.

"Ooooo-kay." He patted my head, then looked at Brooke.

"She normally isn't like this," he said. "I was just going to see what was going on. Ashlee said you asked us not to join you for lunch today. What gives?"

So he was friends with Brooke, Ashlee, and Sydnee, but not me? My outburst clearly made him uncomfortable. My world had turned upside down, and navigating it was proving much harder than I thought possible.

"I'm sorry, Glitch. I just—"

"Glitch?" he asked, his brows sliding together as though I'd grown horns. "Did you just call me Glitch? Is that supposed to be subtle?"

"What? No." My tongue tripped on itself as I tried to explain. "I thought you went by Glitch."

"Why are you even talking to me?" he asked. The brusqueness in his tone brought me up short. The area around us quieted, and every eye turned our way. He looked at Brooke. "And why are you talking to her? I didn't think you associated with anyone who thought she was all that and then some."

"What?" I screeched. Did he know me at all? "Just what are you called, then? Butthead? Because butthead seems to be quite appropriate at the moment."

He nodded. "There she is." He gestured toward Brooke then. "The Lorelei we all know and love to hate. Just don't forget who she is." The sneer he placed on me was full of venom and a deep-seated hatred. It stunned me to my toes.

He turned to leave, saying, "God, this has been the weirdest freaking day."

At that moment, the entire cafeteria grew quiet. I sat down, hoping to avoid any more unwanted attention. Was I just a stone bitch in this alternate reality? I didn't remember turning into a stone bitch.

Luckily, everyone was looking toward the front of the

cafeteria, the line serving pizza. I glanced over my shoulder, and froze. It was Jared. Jared was in my alternate reality. I wanted to run and jump into his arms, too, but that last experience stayed me. Would he know me? He was the Angel of Death. If anyone would remember what happened, it would be him. Whispers erupted around us as I took note of his attire. He was wearing the white T-shirt and jeans he'd first shown up in.

Were we in a time loop? Would it start all over again? Would I be hit by a huge green delivery truck this time, or would it be a small purple Honda?

He turned and started toward our table just like the first time he'd shown up. I pulled my lower lip into my mouth, hoping he'd remember me. Hoping he'd join us and explain what was going on. Instead, he paused when he spotted another student walking up to him. Cameron.

Every muscle in my body flexed in response.

Cameron walked toward him, his gait sure, purposeful. They didn't always get along, so I tensed even more when they met, but Cameron merely leaned in to him and said something quietly. Jared smiled, only it was real. Genuine. Not menacing or threatening like the first time they'd met a few months ago.

Cameron carried a tray over to our table and sat down beside Brooke. Jared followed.

"Hey, you," she said to Cameron, shoving him playfully with her shoulder.

He shoved back. "Hey." Then he glanced over at me, clearly surprised I was sitting there. "Hey, um, Lorelei. This is Jared."

I allowed my gaze to travel up the exquisite length of him until it landed on his dark eyes. They twinkled with appreciation as he held out a hand to me.

"Oh," I said, fumbling to correct my mistake. I took his hand, its warmth spreading through me instantly with the contact. "Nice to meet you."

"He just started here," Brooke said.

"And he's going to make one heck of a football player," Cameron said. "He'll be a great addition to the team."

The shock of that statement had me gawking at him. "You play football?"

Cameron laughed. "Hell no. But Jared here will, right, buddy?"

Buddy? Oh, yeah, I'd entered the Twilight Zone.

"He's already talked to the coach," Cameron continued. "They're drooling. Best stats in the state."

Jared shrugged sheepishly and sat beside me. His thigh brushed up against mine, the contact warm and electric. I was firmly planted in Happyville until I heard Tabitha's heels clicking. It was a sound I'd never forget. I could always tell when she was near, even in my old reality. "Hey, Lor. Thought we'd join you after all."

"Great," Cameron said, his tone condescending. Brooke elbowed him in the ribs as Tabitha and Amber sat down. Whatever had prompted Brooke to ask me to sit with her was clearly going to have to wait.

"I'm Tabitha," she said, holding out her hand to Jared. "Tabitha Sind. And, yes, I do live up to my last name."

I stared wide-eyed at her brazenness. She'd had a thing for him since day one in my old reality, too. Only in this one, Jared seemed to have a thing back. Who could blame him? Tabitha was stunning.

"I'm Amber," her ever-faithful sidekick said. She thought about shaking his hand, too, but Tabitha wouldn't let go of it. She also held his gaze, and he let her for far too long before producing a bashful smile and nodding toward Amber in acknowledgment.

I felt sick. So completely disoriented, I wanted to run home screaming. I didn't like a reality where I was a stone bitch, my best friends either hardly knew me or despised the fact that I dared to breathe, and my boyfriend had eyes for another.

"I'm sorry," I said, a wetness welling between my lashes despite my best efforts. "I'm not feeling well."

I stood and practically ran out of the lunchroom, continued out the front door into the brisk, clean air.

"Can I walk you home?"

I whirled around to the male voice. To Jared's voice. He stood behind me, his brows drawn in concern.

"Jared?"

One corner of his full mouth tilted up and he stepped closer. "That's me. Jared Kovach."

I wanted to ask him if he remembered me, if he remembered what had happened, if we were in heaven, but something stopped me. What if this new reality had rules? What if I broke them? Would I be kicked out? Would I lose my parents again?

"Are you going home?" Tabitha asked. She'd followed Jared, who'd followed me. That girl was truly the bane of my existence, even in heaven. "You'll get in trouble if you don't sign out at the office, but I can drive you if you want me to."

I would much rather have Jared walk me, but I had no delusions that she wouldn't invite herself along.

"I'm okay. I just need some air," I said, unable to tear my gaze off Jared. He had yet to disengage his as well.

"Fine, then. Come on before your food gets cold." She took Jared's arm in hers and led him back inside, and that was about all I could handle of that.

I left the school grounds and hurried down the sidewalks of Riley's Switch toward my home. But when I arrived at my grandparents' store instead, the one that I used to live over, I stopped and stared. Would they be different? Would they be okay?

I'd lost my best friends and my boyfriend in one fell swoop. I didn't think I could take it if I didn't have that un-conditional love I was so used to. I was utterly spoiled where they were concerned, and I was not about to apologize for it.

My parents' house sat about half a mile behind the store, along the tree lines of the mountains. I could see it from where I stood, but I wanted to visit Bill and Vera Lou James. The people who had raised me since I was six. My mother's parents.

Because I was used to doing it, I went around back in-stead of entering through the front and was greeted by the kitchen I'd grown up in. The small, outdated living room sat off to the right and the stairs up to my room to the left.

Grandma's kitchen was filled with all kinds of food as though they were having a cookout or a big party. The party. My party. I had no idea why I was having a party and won-dered if I might should actually ask someone.

Oh, no. That would be too easy. Heaven forbid I do things the easy way.

I called out, but no one answered, so I went through the kitchen and into the store. It was closed. On a weekday. I could read the sign on the door that had been written in black marker.

CLOSED FOR PRIVATE PARTY

That was interesting. Everyone was sure taking the party seriously.

"Hello?" I heard a woman call out.

I went back into the apartment. It was Betty Jo, my grand-mother's best friend.

I beamed at her. "Hi, Betty Jo!" I said, walking toward her.

She held her arms wide. "The big day," she said, giving me one of her Barcalounger hugs. I could always count on Betty Jo for a hug.

"And what a weird day it's been," I said.

She set me at arm's length. "In what way?" she asked, her eyes round with concern. "I mean, everything's okay, right? Still on track?"

"Oh, sure." I nodded, not wanting to worry her, though I had no idea what she was talking about.

A relieved sigh slipped past her lips as she started sorting items into piles of what needed to be refrigerated versus what did not. "Thank God. What a glorious day." The smile she placed on me was full of both appreciation and pride. "You did it, Lorelei. You're amazing."

I blinked in surprise. I hadn't done anything. And her words just brought that to the forefront of my thoughts once again. I hadn't done anything but watch my friends die, only to meet them in heaven that wasn't really a heaven so much as a topsy-turvy version of my old world.

But I couldn't tell her that. She was so . . . grateful. So I nodded and offered her my best Sunday smile instead.

"Do you know where Grandma and Granddad are?"

"Oh—" She looked around. "—I sure don't. But I bet they'll be right back. In fact, they're probably at the church, firing up the grills. You know how your grandfather likes to get a jump start on these things. On a day like today, who can blame him?"

She literally squeaked in excitement and pinched one of my cheeks softly.

I laughed with her, feeling more lost than ever, and said, "Then I'm going upstairs for a minute."

Her brows slid together. "Upstairs?"

"Um, yeah, if that's okay."

"Certainly," she said, a nervous laughter bubbling out of her. "It's just, well, you haven't been upstairs in a very long time."

"Really? Like how long?"

"Oh, I don't know. Never mind me. You go on ahead." She shooed me away with a wave of her hand. "I'll tell your grandmother you're here when she comes in."

"Thanks," I said, already ascending the stairs. When I got to my room, my beautiful, wonderful room, I gasped. It was full of boxes and old furniture. My bed was there, but it had been covered up. My grandparents were using this room as a storage facility. Did I never stay with them anymore?

Sadness tightened around my chest. Sure we were practically neighbors, but even as a kid, I'd stay with my grandparents every chance I got. I could hardly wait for my parents to go out of town for this or that so that I could hang out with Grandma and Granddad. We'd watch movies and eat popcorn until midnight, though we never told my parents that. It was always our secret.

I stepped to the bed and cleared off the multitude of boxes that lay atop it. The comforter was dusty, so I took it in my hands and shook it out. A puff of dust filled the air, causing a sliver of panic to rush through me. It was the war all over again. Clouds of dust swirling around me. My throat started to close as the images forced themselves to the forefront of my every thought. I had to force myself to calm. To slow my heart rate. To relax my muscles.

Then I noticed something. In my memories, the images

of the war were superimposed with other images, other memories, like a double-exposed picture. I saw two realities. When I was looking down at Glitch, at the blood dripping down his face and over his lashes, I saw myself at Tabitha's house as she went on and on about a date she had with a college boy. A college boy who belonged to the Kappa Sigs, whatever that was. But I had to promise not to tell her parents. They'd seriously freak.

"Seriously," Amber said, agreeing with her best friend.

I jolted to awareness, the shock catapulting me out of the memory. A memory that was just surfacing and yet had been there forever, like I'd led two lives. Like I was two different people. I rubbed my eyes, fought the weight of fatigue that had plagued me all day. The weight of sadness that followed me like a ghost.

I lay down on the bed. My bed. The one I'd slept in for a decade.

How could I not visit more often? How could I not be here, in the most sacred place I knew?

My lids felt like lead. I fought to keep them open. I needed to get home and explain to my parents why I'd left school at lunch. They'd be getting a call soon when I was reported absent in sixth hour. I didn't want them to worry. I'd wanted them for so long, what if I fell asleep and they disappeared again? What if this were all a dream?

DUST AND BOXES

Even the horrid likelihood that I would wake up to find out I'd dreamed everything, that my parents weren't really back, that the war hadn't really been diverted, that Glitch and Brooklyn and Cameron and Jared were really still alive, didn't stop my lids from closing and staying closed. They opened only when I heard voices downstairs. They catapulted me out of my slumber and I bolted upright. But I was still here. I was still in this reality, surrounded by dust and boxes. I blinked into the diminishing light. It was late, but I didn't have a phone to check the time.

My parents would be worried.

I scrambled out of the bed and headed for the bathroom to splash water on my face before remembering there wasn't a bathroom. My grandparents had put in a bathroom when I was in the fifth grade. I'd been living with them since I was six, and I'd complained for years about having to go downstairs to use the bathroom in the middle of the night. One weekend my grandmother took me on a shopping trip for school clothes in Albuquerque. We'd even stayed the night in a hotel room. It had a pool and a hot tub and I found the true meaning of happiness that weekend. But when we got back, Granddad and some of his friends had spent the entire weekend putting in a bathroom for me. My very own bathroom. It meant giving up most of my closet, but it was so very worth it.

Now it was back to being a huge closet, almost a room unto itself. Darkness crept in fast, but I didn't want to leave. I sat back down on my bed. Rested my elbows on my knees and my face in the palms of my hands. And the double-exposed picture of my life came back to me. I remembered playing hide-and-seek in this room. It was full of boxes, but at the time, in the other reality, I'd been living in it. Two images formed in my mind, overlapped, melded. Two realities blurring into one.

"The older you got, the more you pulled away."

I jumped at the voice and turned to the doorway. It was my grandfather. My wonderful grandfather with his gray hair and gray eyes and patient smile. He stepped inside, followed by my grandma. Her bright blue irises shone at me. I wanted to run into their arms, but I didn't want to make a fuss. This was a different reality. Somehow, I wasn't just in heaven; I was in more of a parallel universe with overlapping realities that made my head spin.

"From everything you knew," Granddad continued. "Everyone you knew."

My parents were right behind them. They followed them into the small room, and Mom came over to sit beside me, but I had a hard time tearing my gaze away from my grandparents.

"It started when you were very young," Mom said. "You told Casey you hated him."

Casey. I would never get used to calling Glitch Casey.

"And when we asked why, you told us he was going to die anyway. You figured you'd save yourself the pain of losing him later by letting him go then." Mom lowered her head in sadness. "And you hardly spoke to your grandparents, even though they lived right by you. You just pulled away."

Guilt assaulted me as the very grandparents I'd apparently been shunning looked on, their eyes full of more understanding than I deserved.

"You started forming friendships based on how badly the person treated you," Dad said as Mom took my hand in hers.

I frowned as a thought occurred to me. "That would explain my friendship with Tabitha."

"Yes, it would," Grandma said.

Dad kneeled before me. "We just didn't know what to do to help you, Pix. You were so worried about today. Worried you'd failed. Worried you *would* fail."

"Until you hardly ate," Mom said. "Hardly slept. That's why we've been waiting with bated breath for this day to arrive. We knew . . . No, we hoped that things would change. That you would . . . come back to us."

"I'm sorry," I said, tears spilling out over my cheeks.

"No, sweetheart, no," she said, fat tears rushing down her face as well. "You saw so much in those early years. You had so many bad dreams. Saw so many people die. Don't ever be sorry."

"I don't understand what happened. The clouds opened up and thousands of evil spirits escaped onto this plane. I didn't do anything to stop it. I couldn't, no matter how hard I tried."

Granddad grinned. "You're going to have a hell of a time convincing your grandpa Mac of that."

"Mac?" I said. "He's here?"

"Sure is," Mac said from the doorway. "And I thought the party was in the church dining hall. What's everyone doing here?"

"Mac." I brightened. Like always, his presence was a welcoming salve. "You're here."

"Didn't we already cover that?" he asked, his expression shimmering with mirth. "And I brought something for you. Something we agreed on years ago."

He shook out a T-shirt and held it up to me. I read it aloud. "My parents stormed the gates of hell and all I got was this lousy T-shirt."

My voice grew softer and softer as I read. I glanced at my parents, hesitant to talk about what had happened to them. Hesitant to tell them what I'd done. How I'd led them to their deaths. Or, well, their first deaths.

"Then it was real?" I asked. "I didn't dream up an entirely different life? I don't have a split personality?"

"Well, I don't know about that exactly, eh, Bill?" He ribbed Granddad, who laughed right along with him.

He handed me the shirt, and I wadded it into a ball, wishing I could burn the evidence of what I'd done.

"Do you know what happened?" I asked my parents, suddenly unable to meet their eyes.

"We know everything," Mom said. "Well, everything your grandpa Mac would tell us."

Dad frowned at his father before turning back to me. "He's not the most forthcoming sort," he said. "But we got the basic gist of things."

"You were gone for so long," I said, my voice catching on something in my chest.

Mom squeezed my hand. "And we're terribly sorry for that, Pix. We would never have left you on purpose."

"You don't understand," I said, becoming frantic. "There was a wind and this lightning bolt and these clouds and then you were ripped away from me."

Mom flung her arms around me, trying to console us both. "It didn't happen, Pix. It didn't happen, because of what you did."

I leaned back so I could look at her. "I didn't do anything but watch my friends and family die!" My sorrow and terror welled up inside me and threatened to burst out of my chest. "I did nothing."

The bed dipped again as Mac sat next to me. He took my face into his hands, wiped away my tears with the padding of his thumbs. "I beg to differ," he said, his tone matter-of-fact. "You saved the world from total annihilation."

I let a frustrated breath slip through my lips.

Instead of arguing with me, he asked, "Do you remember what we did when I was in prison?"

"You were in prison?" Grandma asked, appalled.

"Apparently," he replied with a grin, teasing her. When I nodded, he said, "Okay, let's try that again. This will be rather new for me, but we've done it before, if memory serves. You told me so."

By this point, I was so confused, I would've agreed to anything if it meant I'd get some answers. "Okay."

He put up a hand, fingers slightly splayed. We had done this when I'd visited him in prison. Only we'd done it through glass and he allowed me to see how he ended up in prison. He'd gone after the men who'd tortured his wife, my grandmother, for information and killed her. The men, descendants of nephilim, had wanted to know about me. My name. My mother's name. Where I was born. They knew the last prophet had been born and wanted to kill me before I had a chance at life. She'd died protecting me. She'd died on the day I was born. Mac went after the men who took her. He killed them all in a shoot-out, received several gunshot wounds in return for his efforts, and almost died himself before he found my paternal grandmother. She was dead, of course. Had been dead for hours. But he held her, rocked her, promised to do the right thing.

The right thing had ended up being prison and making my parents promise never to tell me about him. He thought it would be best. He didn't want his only granddaughter to know the horrors of what he'd done. But I'd found out about him anyway, rather accidentally, actually, when I first found out I could go into pictures. I'd hunted him down, looking for answers, and visited him in prison. And we'd done this very thing. We'd touched hands through the glass. And he showed me everything.

It was a memory I didn't want to relive. When I hesitated, he said, "Pix, history is different. You changed everything."

I swallowed hard and with great effort put my hand on his.

It didn't take long. Images flashed in my mind instantly until he led me to the place he wanted me to see. We were in a field. A wheat field. And a teenaged boy was working on a tractor. I recognized the red hair and kind eyes as being those of my grandfather Mac. It was him as a kid. I looked on in fascination as a girl walked up to him. Me. I walked up to him.

I was wearing the same clothes I'd worn yesterday, during the war. I was filthy. My hair hung in tangles about my face. Dirt smudged my cheeks and forehead, and my clothes were ripped in several places.

Mac looked up from his work, wrench in hand, and stared.

"Mac," I said, praying he'd listen.

Yes, I'd prayed. I remembered my overwhelming sense of fear that he would run or refuse to listen after I'd struggled so hard to get there. To get to him.

Realization of what happened catapulted me back to the present. I gasped and reeled as my surroundings blurred and shifted into my old room. Lowering my hand, I took a moment to absorb the new memories bombarding me; then I gazed at Mac, stunned to my toes.

"I did it," I whispered. "I went into the picture Glitch had in his hand. It was of you."

Mac smiled and nodded, and Mom wrapped an arm around me.

"Your mother took that picture when you weren't looking," I continued. "She'd been given a new camera for her birthday, and you were her first subject. Her very first picture."

Mac's brows shot up. "You saw all that?" he asked.

"Yes, but—" I blinked and thought back. "—but I didn't get a good look at her. She was behind the camera. I couldn't get past it. Wait a minute." I beamed at him as a new realization emerged. "You saw me. Most people can't see me when I go into pictures."

"I'm not most people."

A soft, bewildered laugh escaped me. "You certainly aren't. You saw me. Just like Jared does when I go into that other picture."

"I did see you. And let me tell you, you scared the shit out of me at first."

I laughed again, only this time in nervousness. Granddad would clobber me if I used that word in his presence. Apparently he wouldn't do the same to Grandpa Mac. Thank goodness. I was fairly certain Mac could take him. "You're like a prophet, too. You have abilities, but you're male."

He nodded. "It's true. Most of the males in the line have some small amount of extrasensory perception, but we are nothing compared to the women in our family. Our feminine counterparts are gifted beyond measure."

Grandma sat on a box in front of me. "You changed everything," she said reassuringly. "You changed the future. You stopped the war."

"But how?" I asked, still not quite understanding.

"You told me everything that day," Mac said. Then he held up his hand again. "Want to see?"

I filled my lungs, put my hand on his again, and dived back into the past. It took me a while to convince Mac of who I was, but he'd grown up knowing about the prophecies and the texts. He knew about the possibility of a female being born in his lifetime. Of the impending war. So what I told him wasn't so foreign he couldn't comprehend. Couldn't believe. But it did take a while.

I told him everything. I didn't know how much time I had, but we walked through the wheat field as the sun set and I told him all about his wife, how he would meet her, how he would fall in love. Then I told him everything after that. I told him the bad stuff. Everything I could think of before I ran out of time and was killed in the war.

After our long talk, we looked back. Mac's mother was still aiming the camera. The sun was still hanging in the same position, even though it seemed like hours later. Time had not passed.

He looked at me like one would something they loved. "These are the end times," he said. "And we have the power to change the world."

I nodded. "Please, Mac, please save your wife. My parents. If you do nothing else, please save them. Tell my dad not to go to the ruins that day."

This time my surroundings melted more slowly. I didn't want to leave. My grandfather as a teen boy was so handsome and strong and I trusted him implicitly. I'd placed the fate of the world in his hands.

After I reemerged back into the present, I questioned him with a quirk of my brow. "How did you stop it all?" I asked him in awe. I'd told him what was going to happen, but he would still have to stop it all. How?

"I followed your directions," he said, grinning. "I ran home and wrote everything down as fast as I could. Dates. Names. Events. Then, when the time came, I warned people what was about to happen. I stopped your friend Cameron's mother from going on a bike ride that you said would end in tragedy."

Cameron's mother? He'd saved her life?

"I went on a camping trip with Casey's Boy Scout troop when he was in second grade, kept a constant vigil on him, and stopped, I'm assuming, whatever happened to him."

And I'd never found out what that was. When Glitch was in the second grade, his troop went on a camping trip during spring break. Something happened. I never found out what, but it had changed Glitch. He withdrew, became depressed, and hated—no, more like feared—Cameron from that day on. That would explain why they were now friends when in the other reality they could hardly stand each other. But I was still dying to know what happened on that trip.

"And most important," Mac continued, "I stopped the men who took my wife."

"She's alive?" I asked, hope blossoming in my chest.

Mac lowered his gaze. "No, ma'am, she is not."

"But—"

Grandma put a hand on my knee to shush me. "She died of cancer a few years ago, but you knew her."

"That's right," Dad said. "If you'll think back to your memories of this time, you knew her."

I tried to remember. It would come to me, I was sure of it. My new past was revealing itself bits at a time.

"But she's here with us in spirit," Mac said, so sure of it, there was no sadness in his voice. "And I stopped Dyson."

"Dyson?" I asked with a gasp.

"Pix," he said, lowering his gaze again. "Before it got to that, enough things came to pass for me to know that everything you said was the God's honest truth." He chewed on his lower lip before admitting, "I did what I had to do."

"You . . . you killed him?" I asked.

"Yes, ma'am, between you, me, and the fence post, I did. Mr. Jake Dyson, aka Norman Sydow, died in a home invasion about fifteen years ago. I saw no reason to let someone like that live. He'd already been cooking up a plan. He had a book called a grimoire. He knew how to open the gates. Knew how to summon a demon and was researching exactly which one he wanted to summon."

"Malak-Tuke," I said.

"He hadn't settled on any one at the time of his death, but yes, that name was on his list."

"Then you stopped him from opening the gates in the first place." I looked at my parents in turn. "You saved them."

"No, Pix," Mac said. "You did. Just like our ancestors prophesied, you stopped the war before it ever happened."

"No," I said, disagreeing completely, "not just me. All of us." Every single one of my friends had been involved in saving the world. Brooke with her insistence that I practice, that I learn to go into pictures and hone my skills. Jared fighting the demons off before they could come after me, before they could stop the prophecy from coming to fruition. Cameron protecting me as long as he possibly could, long enough for the picture to end up in my hands. Kenya going back for said picture, that handful of photographs of no importance whatsoever. Then Glitch giving his life to retrieve just one, the one that would change the world.

We did the impossible. All of us together.

I shook out the T-shirt and pulled it over my V-neck before looking at my parents. "You don't know how long I've dreamed of this. And it's not that I don't appreciate everything, but what the heck is this party about?"

"Didn't you see that part?" Mac asked me.

"I don't think so." I scanned my brain. "Nope. No idea."

"You told me the date."

"The date?"

"The date of the war. You told me when it would happen and you said if we were still alive the next day, aka today, then we'd done it. We'd stopped the war. Then you insisted," he added, seeming to hold back a chuckle, "with your torn clothes and dirty face, that we were to throw a huge party to celebrate. You didn't have much faith when you appeared to me. You were so lost, so desperate. But you said if this day came, if we made it this far, we had to celebrate and that you wanted this very T-shirt." He pointed to my new T-shirt.

I let out a throaty laugh of astonishment. "Do you think we really stopped it?" I asked them.

Dad took my shoulders into his large hands. "Lorelei Pixie Stick McAlister," he said, shaking me a little.

I loved it when he called me that.

"You did it. We made it. We are here and we're alive because of you."

"And my friends," I added.

"And your friends. It's time to stop worrying."

Mom nodded and squeezed me against her. "And no more bad dreams."

"Bad dreams? Of the war?"

She nodded.

"So even though the war had supposedly been thwarted, I still had the dreams?"

"We think that, perhaps, you were reliving a different life somehow," she said. "Your other life."

Grandma sniffed into a handkerchief and added, "You're very powerful, Lorelei. Your abilities far exceeded even our expectations. You've been seeing that life since you were a kid."

"We didn't understand it at first," Dad said. "And nothing we did seemed to help, so we just waited."

"For this day," Granddad said.

Mac tugged on a lock of hair. "For this marvelous, glorious day." He started to rise, then stopped and added, "And for the food. The food is always a plus."

He slipped my hands into his to help me up.

"I'm sorry about Grandma Olivia," I said, truly and deeply sad about the death of his wife. "If only I'd known that, too. I really wanted to get to know her better."

"Me, too, Pix, but she was so proud of you. Never forget that."

THE MAGIC
DISSOLVING-BONES TRICK

Cameron had started a bonfire behind the church. When we pulled up, there were several students out there whose parents were part of the Order. Some I recognized. Some I didn't. I walked out to join them as my parents went inside to lay out more food for the feast. Overall, the mood was terribly somber for such a festive event.

"Hey, Lorelei," Brooklyn said to me as I strolled up, not really certain I should join them. She was sitting by a brooding Cameron. It would seem the Cameron I knew and loved like one loved a thug with the ability to snap people's necks in the blink of an eye was back. I couldn't help but notice the odd glances people were casting my way as they walked past carrying in food. They were doing the same to Cameron.

"Hey, Brooke," I said, and she looked at me in surprise. No idea why. She'd said hi to me first.

I noticed Glitch had come, probably because his father was a member of the Order and had dragged him here. He walked away and disappeared into the shadows of the building when I joined them. The thought of Glitch and me being at odds was the most foreign thing about this entire day. Having my parents back after they'd been missing for ten years? Awesome. Knowing I'd gone through a picture and told my paternal grandfather how to save the world? Worked for me. But Glitch and me at odds? Disliking each other? Not hanging out? Not ordering pizza and watching '80s movies all weekend? No way. I just couldn't see it. It felt wrong on a thousand levels.

I was beginning to remember this life, though. Snippets of time revealed themselves to me slowly. I tried to remember when I'd pushed him away. What I'd done. But it wouldn't surface. It was there. I'd get it eventually, but for now, I would just have to wing it. To make amends based on second-hand knowledge.

"No one ever calls me that," Brooke said, and I realized she was talking about my calling her Brooke.

I closed my eyes in frustration. Another misstep. "I'm sorry."

"No," she said, rushing to reassure me. "It's okay. I love it. It was just . . . I don't know, a surprise."

She frowned into the fire then, as though her thoughts had gotten the best of her. Then she explained. "It's like

I remember you calling me Brooke even though we've never been friends."

I took a mental step back. Was she starting to remember our other life? Our other reality?

I jumped to sit on her other side, hoping she'd elaborate.

But Cameron spoke then, seeming just as confused, just as lost. "I remember stuff, too. Stuff that never happened, only I remember it like it did."

"Like a double-exposed picture," I said, encouraging him.

He fixed his gaze on me. "You know what I am." He said it accusingly.

Brooke frowned at him. "What you are?"

But Cameron's gaze never left mine.

Before I could answer, before I could explain, a woman walked up to us. She had soft blond hair and kind eyes, and I knew her. I knew her from somewhere.

"Food's ready," she said to all of us; then she ruffled Cameron's hair. He didn't seem to mind, which surprised me even more.

After she walked away, it hit me. "Holy cow, Cameron, that was your mother."

He nodded. "Why does that surprise you?"

His mother had died when he was three. It was a constant source of pain for him. He'd been there. He'd watched her fall to her death. She'd sacrificed her life for him, and Jared was the one who came for her. Being what he was, part angel and part human, Cameron saw him when others would not have. He'd never forgotten Jared, which was the root cause of their initial strife. And probably a lot of it afterwards as well.

"It doesn't. I just didn't recognize her. It's been a long time since I've seen her."

He bit down, worked his jaw. "You're lying."

"Cameron," Brooke said. "That's not nice."

"Maybe not nice," he said, shooting daggers at me with his gaze. "But true. Because my mother is not supposed to be here."

Brooke's brows slid together. "You're right," she said. "I remember that, too. She died when you were a baby."

Cameron, in a rare show of emotion, scraped a hand over his face, then held it there. He squeezed Brooke's hand with the other as he tried to regain control of himself. I could sense the pain rushing through him as he remembered his mother's death.

"But that was a different time," I said, putting my arm across Brooke and rubbing their hands reassuringly. "A time that has been altered. It never happened. I guess. I'm not really sure how it works."

His breath hitched in his chest, and emotion, strong and potent, seeped out of him. He was crying. Sobbing behind his hand. My shock could not have been more evident if I'd screamed it from the rooftops.

Brooklyn threw her arms around him, tears stinging her eyes, too.

"How is this possible?" she asked, and I wondered how many more would remember two realities. Only those most affected? That would definitely include us. And most of the people in Riley's Switch.

"How do I know," Brooke continued, "that you're an angel?"

Cameron's gaze snapped to hers, his eyes red, his lashes glittering and spiked with wetness.

She nodded. "You are. I remember. And so do they." She pointed to the newest members to arrive. They also walked past us with curiosity burning in their gazes.

Cameron didn't say anything. Obviously, not everyone in the Order had known about him before this. But they'd learned what he was in the other reality. They'd had to.

Having been watching us, Glitch stepped out of the shadows, his stance guarded, his shoulders at an angle as though ready to run.

"We were best friends," he said to me accusingly. "We'd been best friends since we could walk, and you just tossed me aside. But before, in the place of our memories, we were still best friends. We did everything together."

He was hurt and not willing to forget what I'd done. Unfortunately, I still didn't remember myself. But it was coming to me. Why I'd pushed my best friend away. Why I withdrew into a shell, a wizard's curtain of indifference and arrogance. And I remember yelling at him in first grade. We were on the playground and he'd accidently spilled his drink on my shirt. I railed at him. It was the excuse I'd been waiting for. I railed at him and pushed him away from me. When he tried to apologize, I did the unthinkable. I slapped him, and I did it in front of the whole school. Everyone laughed, but my heart was breaking. I just wanted him away from me. I didn't want to love him. If I'd failed, if the world was going to end, I didn't even want to know his name.

I was beginning to remember my dreams. Why, even as a child, I knew what was going to happen—the opening of the gates, the war, the end of the world—in the first place. I had been dreaming my whole life of the life I'd altered. The life I'd changed. I knew in my heart it was real. Everything I'd been dreaming was real.

I stood and faced him. If anyone deserved an answer, he did.

"I love you so much," I said, shame and sympathy burning

my face. "I was so afraid. I remember now. I was afraid that whatever I'd done, or tried to do, had failed." I stepped to him and placed my hand on his beautiful face. He glared at me in distaste, but allowed me to stay close. "I've loved you since the first time I saw you."

"We were in diapers."

"I remember. And I loved you even then."

"You're really good at hiding it."

"It would seem so," I said, nodding, ashamed.

He shook off my hand and stuffed his own into his pockets. "I can remember doing things with you. Things that never happened, and yet I can remember doing them. It's like a dream swirling in my head."

"Me, too," Brooke said. "I remember so much. Little snippets of life keep revealing themselves like memories I'd forgotten. Like a past life that I could only recall under hypnosis."

Cameron wiped at his face and stared into the fire. He looked like he used to. Restless. Angry. Guarded. "My mother died," he said, his voice echoing with resentment. "I remember her dying. I remember him—" He glared at the flames. "—I remember the reaper coming for her." He shook his head, unable to completely accept what we were saying. "Azrael. How is that even possible?"

All of us at once realized someone else was close by. We looked over at Cameron's mother. She'd brought him a plate of food. It hung limp in her hands, its contents on the verge of spilling over the side. And like us, she was staring off into space as though being bombarded with memories of things that had never happened.

In fact, everyone at the party seemed to be remembering a different reality than what they'd enjoyed the last few years. I wondered how many in the world would remember a different past. Was it only us? Did we somehow rate the memories of a life we supposedly never lived? Or would everyone remember?

Most people spoke softly to one another, reminiscing about things that never quite happened. They looked at me in awe. In utter amazement. I was the prophet. That much they knew. But now they knew something had changed, and they believed I'd caused it. But I hadn't. We had. All of us.

Brooke stood and took my hand into hers. "I remember something else, too. I remember I loved you with all my heart and soul."

I lowered my head, embarrassed by the sudden onset of tears. They quaked on my lower lashes, big and fat, threatening to spill over.

"I remember you were like the sun to me. You were like air. I've never loved a friend more than you. And I'm pretty sure I never will again."

She pulled me into a hug that wrenched a sob from my throat. I needed that hug so bad. I wanted her in my life. In this life as well as any others that might crop up here or there. Admittedly, I didn't want to live any more lives. Two was enough. But anything without Brooke in it was not a life for me.

Cameron stood and went to his mother, led her back inside the dining hall. He deposited her, consoled her with a kiss on the cheek, then came back out, and I quickly realized why. Someone was standing behind me. Close behind me. I felt a finger run down my arm and across my palm. I didn't turn. I knew exactly who it was. The only person who made the bones in my legs dissolve.

I leaned back into him, and he stepped closer. Molded his body to mine. I melted against him, my hips tucked into the bend at his as he wrapped an arm around my waist and locked me to him. He bent and nuzzled an ear while whispering in it. It caused a rush of excitement over my skin.

"I wasn't sure what you'd remember at first," he said, his voice deep and soft and smooth. "I wanted to give you some time."

"I didn't remember any of this life at first. Only the other one. The one we changed."

He turned me around to face him, and I wasn't about to let him go. I locked my arms around him and looked up, way up, into his darkly shimmering eyes.

"I'm surprised," he said, seeming, well, surprised. "I thought you'd forget that life for a while. I didn't know if you'd ever remember it, remember us, so I decided to start school all over again." He grinned, and it shot through me like an arrow. "I had every intention of wooing you all over again."

I laughed, so relieved and thrilled to have him in my arms again, I felt giddy for the first time that day. Usually, giddy was rather normal for me. "It wouldn't have taken much," I said.

Jared looked up as Cameron stepped to us, his expression challenging, and I wanted to groan aloud. He had sensed Jared coming. He could do that. They both could do that. Sense each other from afar. It was apparently an angel thing.

"I was willing to forgive what you are when you first showed up," Cameron said. "But not now, Reaper."

Darn it. We were back to calling Jared Reaper.

He started to step toward him, but his mother walked back out again. She walked right up to Jared and put her hand on his face as though she were dreaming. I knew the feeling. "I remember," she said. "I prayed that you'd come for me, that you'd save Cameron, and you did."

"Mom, go back inside," Cameron said.

She ignored him and kept staring. Kept touching his face. Jared didn't mind, but her son did not share that kind of patience. He pulled her away from him and stepped close.

"Cameron," I said, getting between them. "If you'll remember what happened the last time you two fought, you'll know that you're not going to hurt him."

Jared spoke softly behind me, clearly amused. "No, it hurt. Just not for long."

I pressed my mouth and started over. "You're not going to kill him."

"I don't want to kill him," Cameron said, squishing me as he pressed forward. "Where's the fun in that?" He had morphed into the old Cameron. His transformation was complete. I wasn't sure how I should feel about that.

"Son!" Cameron's dad came out.

He was so different from Cameron. Where Cameron was tall and blond with ice blue eyes, Cameron's dad was stocky, dark, with eyes so dark, they looked black. His mother was blond, though, but I was certain he got most of his attributes from his actual father, the archangel Jophiel. That was the one thing you could always count on in a nephilim. Extreme height. Cameron had supernatural strength and speed to go with it, all the better to do his job, I supposed.

Mr. Lusk tugged at his son, then glanced at Jared and nodded. "Your Grace," he said, his tone reverent.

Cameron's, not so much. "If the war was really stopped," he said, "then why are you still here?"

And that was quite possibly the biggest mystery in all of

this. If we'd won, if we'd truly changed the past and stopped the war before it ever started, then why was he here? I hadn't wanted to ask it, not even internally, I was so grateful for the fact that he was. That he'd stayed or come back. Whatever he'd done, he was still the most beautiful thing on two legs.

Everyone came out to watch the showdown. They poured out of the dining hall, my parents and grandparents included. And the sheriff who might or might not remember Jared was on our side.

"We won, right?" someone asked. It was Brooklyn's mom, a beautiful African American woman, tiny with spiked hair and a button nose I'd always loved. Comparing her to her husband was much like comparing Mr. Lusk to Cameron. Her husband was tall and pale, thin and very handsome. "Lorelei did it."

He started to answer, but I interrupted. "No, I didn't." I gestured to everyone standing around me. "We did. All of us together, including a girl named Kenya from Maine. And of course, my granddad Mac."

Mac offered me a sheepish grin.

"He did all the hard work."

"I could never have done it without you. What you kids did," he began, but he had to pause and gather himself. After a moment, he said, "What you kids did was extraordinary. The memories of that time are coming back to us. To all of us."

"But, it won't happen again, right?" she asked again. "It's over. The prophecies have come to pass."

Jared nodded. "They have come to pass. My brethren are calling it the War that Never Was and Never Will Be. I think that's a pretty good indication of things to come."

Relief washed over every face there. My grandparents looked at me with stars in their eyes, and I still couldn't believe how I'd treated them in this reality. I had a lot to make up for and I looked forward to every minute of it.

"Then why are you still here?" Cameron said, pushing the subject, his anger still not quite abated.

"It's a gift," he said, staring down at me. Then he looked at everyone. "If you'll have me, I have been given permission to live among you. Something about bravery in battle. I can live as one of you, be human. Kind of. I can't grow old." Then he cast his gaze toward the ground as though suddenly unsure. "So they fixed that, too," he said softly. His next words were so soft, I barely heard them. "Be still."

I looked around and realized he'd stopped time. We were the only ones moving. Grandpa Mac stood with a soda halfway to his mouth. Betty Jo had a corn on the cob at hers, and Mr. Gibson, one of the church elders, had dropped his plate. It hung frozen in the air, his expression comedic.

"If you so choose," Jared said as though uncertain, drawing me back to him, "you will be immortal with me."

"Immortal?" I asked, stunned into an overwhelming state of confusion.

"We have been together for centuries anyway, they figured we might as well stay that way."

"I still don't understand when you say that. How have we been together for centuries?"

"It's hard to explain, because it hasn't actually happened yet. But you've been visiting me since the beginning of time. We fell in love millions of years ago."

While I didn't doubt that in the least—I'd learned not to doubt—I could question. I had lots of those. "How?"

His charming grin sent tiny shivers lacing down my spine. "You'll figure it out. You are a goddess of time, after all. You've done something no one else in human history has ever done. You traveled into the past and stopped the war that would end all wars. Let's just say, the higher-ups are impressed. But this is a limited-time offer. You have to either accept or deny me."

I pushed my mouth to one side in thought. "I don't know. This is a big decision."

He chuckled and waited patiently, knowing exactly what I was going to do. I rolled onto my toes. "Yes and yes and yes again."

"Done."

I closed my eyes, waiting to feel different. Waiting to feel immortal. It was more than I'd ever hoped for. But I didn't feel any different, and the noises around us restarted. Everyone came back to life.

Jared leaned down and put his mouth at my ear. "You'll have to trust me on this. We may have to move often. I'm not sure how immortals will be looked upon."

Laughing, I pulled him closer, reveled in the feel of him against me. Power emanated from every beautiful cell in his body.

My granddad walked up then, so I broke my hold and beamed at him. He'd been the patriarch of the Order the entire time I was growing up, but he'd basically taken over for my father. Now, Grandpa Mac was the minister and Granddad was a deacon. It suited him.

He put out his hand. Jared took it into his own.

"You're welcome to stay," Granddad said.

With a relieved smile, Jared said, "I appreciate that."

Everyone else nodded as well, some a little more hesitantly than others, but there seemed to be a majority. Until we got to Cameron. He held out his hand and I tensed, not sure what he would do when Jared took it.

He stepped close and said, "She's still my responsibility. This doesn't change anything. And I can still kick your ass."

The patient smile Jared wore morphed into something mischievous and slightly evil. "Care to test that theory?"

He removed his coat. Cameron removed his. And I dropped my head into my hands. This was so not going to end well.

Brooke came to stand beside me as they started the War that Was and Will Always Be.

"This all seems very familiar," she said, her brows drawn in thought.

"Yes." I put my arm around her. "Yes, it is."

POTATO SALAD AND WAR

All in all, they were pretty well matched. It only reminded me a little bit of the battle they'd fought when Jared showed up the first time. In that one, they'd done their darnedest to destroy downtown Riley's Switch. This time, instead of two-by-fours and tire irons, they seemed a little more focused on choke holds and knees to the face. Their desire to be close to each other was sweet.

After they knocked a hole in the side of the building, Granddad made them take it outside. When Cameron pointed out that they *were* outside, Granddad replied with, "*More* outside," and pointed to the forest.

And that was exactly the direction Cameron flew after a solid kick from Jared sent him that way. Funny thing was, they were both enjoying every minute of it. I would never understand them.

Most stayed to watch the small war. Some went home to be alone with their families, their fears quieted, and some went back inside for more food. Though we couldn't see much of the actual action, the sounds were quite entertaining. Bones crunching. Trees cracking. And every once in a while, the air would be filled with the deep laugh of whoever had just gotten in the best punch or kick.

Glitch fixed Brooklyn and me a plate, then sat outside with us to watch the fire and listen to the groans of agony emanating from the forest. It was a peace offering and it was nice. Grandpa Mac joined us, cringing every so often at a particularly loud crack, unable to tell if it was bone or branch.

I turned to him. "Did you ever find out why Dyson started it? Why he wanted to open the gates in the first place?"

Mac lowered his head. "He was a distant relation of yours," he said, and I could tell he hadn't wanted to. "I knew we would have to have this conversation, no matter how much I was hoping to avoid it."

"A relation?" I asked.

"Do you remember the story of Arabeth?" he asked me.

"Absolutely. She had a vision that the well water in her village was tainted. Worried for the safety of the townspeople, she ran to warn them. And they burned her for it."

"Yes, but her pain mostly came from the betrayal of her husband. He turned against her when she needed him most."

"I remember."

"Well, he had other children with another woman. It was from that line that Dyson descended. The husband had retained many of Arabeth's documents. Among them was a grimoire. She never used it. Said its power would sour the user. Would foul the mind. Dyson had inherited it along with some other of Arabeth's other writings. He had it translated and he realized what it was. He started using the spells it contained and, well, started turning his life around. He got very rich very fast and he figured, why stop there?"

"So all this boiled down to two lines of descendants that had never stopped fighting."

"That's my take on it. Oh, and there was someone in there looking for you." He glanced over his shoulder. "Found her!"

Ms. Mullins walked out of the dining hall, carrying a plate and a red Solo cup.

"Thanks," she said, clearly not meaning it.

"Sorry, I got sidetracked."

She looked in horror toward the forest. "I can see that. What on earth?"

I patted to an empty chair next to me. "Boys. They're all crazy."

"Except me," Glitch said.

Brooke scoffed. "If I'm remembering things correctly, and I'm pretty sure I am, you once believed turtles were going to take over the world."

"I still do," he said, completely serious. "They have beady eyes and sharp beaks."

I was just about to ask what that had to do with world domination, but Mac interrupted.

"What did you say?" he asked Glitch. He seemed astounded by something Glitch said.

"Turtles," he repeated after taking another bite of his

burger. "They're going to take over the world. I saw it in a dream when I was a kid. Also, one bit me once. They bite hard and it got really infected. I hate them." He took a drink of his orange soda, then continued. "I hate them all."

Brooke fought a grin as Mac said, "That's amazing."

That got our attention. "What?" we asked in unison.

"You may find this a really bizarre coincidence, but Dyson's real name was Norman Terrapin-Sydow. He dropped the Terrapin early on, then later changed his name entirely to Jake Dyson. But terrapin, it's a species of freshwater turtles. He changed his name after he got into some trouble back East. That's why it took me a while to locate him. He went by Terrapin for most of his life."

"See!" Glitch said, thrilled that he was right all along. "What'd I tell you?"

"He even had a huge tattoo of a turtle on his back."

Brooke and I blinked, a tad horrified that Glitch had been right all along.

"I win," he said, taking another bite. "Don't ever doubt me, girls. You'll live to regret it, I promise."

Brooke turned to me, still in shock. "Is this going to go to his head?"

"Oh, yeah," I said. "We could be in some real trouble."

"Was that a human?" Ms. Mullins asked, her eyes wide in alarm.

"Probably," I said to her. "They'll be okay. They do this all the time."

She nodded, lifted a forkful of potato salad to her mouth, then let it hover there as she listened to another crack followed by a loud groan. But the part that really seemed to horrify her was the evil laugh that drifted toward us.

I wasn't sure if I should tell her or not, but since the war was basically over, having never been started, I didn't think it would hurt anything. I leaned over to her and said quietly, "I know you're the observer."

She put her fork down. "How did you know?" she asked, her eyes shimmering in the firelight.

"Are you remembering like all the others?"

After she sighed haplessly, she said, "I am. I wasn't sure what to say. What to report to the Vatican."

"If you don't want to tell them I know, don't. I'm not going to tell anyone. Unless they remember from the other reality, no one but me will be aware of your position."

"So," Dad said as he came out and crouched down between us. "The observer, huh?"

Mac blinked in surprise. "You're the observer?"

"She sure is. And a darned good one, from what I'm told." He patted her back. "Welcome to the fold. Now that you'll be kicked out, we'll always have a place for you."

He gave me a quick kiss on the cheek, frowned in the general direction of the sound of a tree falling, then went back inside.

I looked that way, too. "Never mind."

Ms. Mullins finally put the fork in her mouth, chewed a moment, then said, "It was fun while it lasted."

I felt bad. They would replace her now, though I had no idea why. What else could happen?

Tabitha pulled up then, her stereo blaring, her sports car flashing red even in the low light as she slammed the door and marched toward me. Straight toward me. Fists on hips. Mouth forming a thin line of anger.

"You didn't," she said, then paused for dramatic effect before adding, "come over. I had no idea what to wear to this stupid party."

I stood and took Brooke's and Glitch's plates before turning toward the dining hall. Brooke winked at me mirthfully. "Sorry, Tab. I was a little busy."

"Too busy for me? Your best friend? Your go-to girl?"

I walked to the trash barrel just outside the dining hall, tossed in the plates, then turned back to her. "How come we're best friends only when you want to be best friends?"

She gestured to herself. "Duh."

Offering up a quick prayer for patience, I said, "You know what? I think we should break up."

"Break up?" she shrieked, following me into the hall. "You're breaking up with me? With *me*?"

If anything could bring conversations to a screeching halt, it was a teenaged girl having a hissy fit. Admittedly, Tabitha wasn't that bad once you got to know her. I had some fond memories that, thankfully, I wasn't present for, but some relationships just weren't meant to be.

"It's not you," I said, heading toward the drinks table. "It's me. I just think we need some space. You know, see other people."

"I—I don't know what to say. I feel violated."

"Would iced tea help?" I asked, pointing toward the tea cooler.

"No, iced tea won't help!"

If anyone would try the patience of Job, it was Tabitha Sind. But there was a side to her that not very many people saw. It made me question everything. I'd apparently become a bitch to keep people at a distance. Did Tabitha do the same thing?

It was a possibility, especially when taking into account that something that had happened to her a year earlier. Something only I'd known about. Something I'd seen in one of my more horrid visions. But we were in a different reality now. Did it still happen? Better yet, could I still see? I opened the spout and let fresh iced tea stream into my cup. I hadn't had a vision since the switch to Supernatural Savings Time.

In an attempt to hide what I was doing, I coughed into my hand and took hold of Tabitha's arm, pretending to use her for balance. I drew in a deep breath and concentrated. For my efforts, I experienced her horror, her utter shame and self-loathing, once again. Her future had not been changed. She'd fallen into the same trap as before. Been dealt the same unfair hand.

The world tipped, and I found myself fighting for balance when I felt a strong arm around my waist once again. I clutched on to Jared's shirt as Tabitha, completely ignoring me, flashed her million-dollar smile at him.

The one positive thing that came of that little experience was that I did control the vision to a degree. I'd searched for it. Unfortunately, I found it, but I was getting stronger still. I could hone my visions to see what I wanted to see when I wanted to see it. The visions would no longer control me.

Nah, who was I kidding? I could hardly control my own addiction to orange soda, much less something as powerful as a supernatural gift. But it was a nice thought. And at least I could control it to some degree.

Jared growled, and I realized I'd just lied to myself. Two positive things came out of my snooping around Tabitha's past. I got Jared's arms around me again.

"Oh, hey, Jared," Tabitha said, her tone suddenly syrupy sweet.

"Hey," he said with a nod, his breaths heavy, labored. He set me right, waited a minute to make sure I could stand on my own, then brushed past me, literally brushing past me.

Every part of his body that could touched mine as he stepped to the water cooler and poured himself a cup. He winked at me from behind it, and that's when I noticed the blood and bruises that covered pretty much every inch of him.

I was quick. Nothing got past me.

"I hope you're faring better than your opponent," I said, trying to contain my mirth. A few weeks ago, I would have been horrified, but I'd learned to let Jared and Cameron be, well, Jared and Cameron. Apparently supernatural beings needed more playtime than humans. And roughness helped, too.

Jared downed the water, then went for another cup. "He's writhing in agony," he said as it streamed out of the cooler. "I decided he was taking too long to recover and came in for a drink to pass the time."

"Good to know you're worried about him."

He fixed a brilliant smile on me, downed the second cup, then asked, "You think I should take him some water?"

"That would be nice."

He tossed the cup with a wicked laugh. When I narrowed my eyes on him, he said, "You didn't see what he did with that tree branch. Some things are just wrong. He doesn't deserve water."

I grinned and he bent down and kissed my cheek before heading back out.

"You can do better than that," I said, teasing him with a smirk.

He turned back around, still out of breath, and took a good long look at me, starting at the top of my head and ending at the tips of my toes. Then he stepped back to me.

"I'm all dirty and bloody and stuff."

"Exactly how I like my men."

His brows shot up. "Your men?" he asked, taking the hem of my shirt into his hand and drawing me closer. "Just how many men do you have?"

"Oh, a plethora." I waved his question off as though it were simply too difficult to give an exact number.

"Ah," he said, nodding in understanding. "That's a lot. But can they do this?"

He wrapped me in his arms and bent me backwards. I felt my feet slide off the floor and clutched on to him for balance. Then, in an act of pure pleasure, he put his lips on mine. Warm and pliant, they molded to my mouth, his breath mingling with mine. He seemed to lose himself. He plunged one hand into my hair and pulled me tighter as he angled his head and deepened the kiss.

My insides stirred with his touch, with his tongue delving into my mouth, with the fierceness with which he seemed to want to devour me. Without breaking the kiss, he straightened and pulled me off the floor. A soft growl escaped his throat as his mouth left mine and trailed tiny kisses to my ear and down my neck. I'd never felt anything quite like it.

Someone cleared a throat. Someone close. I let my eyes drift open and saw Granddad standing in front of me.

"Granddad!" I cried, reality crashing through like a dousing of ice water.

Jared set me on the floor instantly, keeping hold so I didn't topple over. Then we both turned toward my grandfather, who seemed . . . annoyed. For some reason.

"Hey, Granddad. Jared was just demonstrating the Heimlich maneuver. You know, in case I ever come across someone choking."

"Unless you mean choking on someone else's tongue, I don't think that particular maneuver will help."

Cameron shouted from a distance. "What are you doing? Get back out here, you wuss! You hit like a girl!"

"Hey!" Brooklyn shouted in protest. "There's nothing wrong with hitting like a girl!"

Granddad cleared his throat again. Jared took that as his cue to leave. He stepped past my glaring grandfather but turned back to me, let his gaze linger as he pulled his bottom lip into his mouth. I kind of melted. Until Granddad stepped into my line of sight again.

"The food was great," I said, my buoyant tone ringing false even to myself. "Did I mention that yet?"

Thankfully almost everyone had gone home by that point, but an exact account of tonight's happenings would still be making the rounds by Sunday's sermon. No telling what it would be on.

"You need to see to your friend."

For a split second I wondered whom he was talking about. Then I remembered Tabitha. I swung around. She stood staring at me wide-eyed.

Raising one shoulder in a gesture of innocence, she asked, "So, um, are you seeing Jared?"

Subtle. "No, we're just friends. Are you okay?"

Relief washed over her visibly. She believed me. Goodness.

"I'm fine," she said. "I just wonder if maybe I should ask him out."

For all her bravado, I realized that she hadn't actually seen anyone in over a year, and now I knew why. Despite everything, I felt sorry for her.

"Yes, Tabitha," I said, trying to break it to her gently, "we're seeing each other. I would've thought it obvious." Well, not too gently.

She crinkled her nose and gave me a measuring once-over. "Well, it shouldn't be hard to lure him away. Considering."

And I was feeling sorry for her. Wow.

But still, what I'd seen before was more than a little disturbing. I tried to remember that as she bounced away. I followed her out the door and sat back down beside my new old best friends. We'd done it. Together we'd done it.

"I have to ask you," Brooke said, pulling me out of my thoughts. "Can you still do . . . you know. Am I remembering correctly? All the things you used to do? All the times I forced you to practice? Is that still a go?"

I didn't want to tell her I was just wondering the same thing. "Oh, my God," I said instead, exaggerating my annoyance. "Practice, practice, practice. That was your mantra twenty-four/seven."

She got defensive. I tried not to laugh. "Well, practice makes perfect. Where would you be without me?"

"Where would any of us be without you?"

A satisfied smirk lit her face, but quickly disappeared. Her gaze slid past me in thought. "It's crazy," she said. "We've lived two lives. How many people can say that?"

"Not many."

She bounced back then elbowed me. "Thank God, right?"

I laughed. "Definitely, thank God."

Another car pulled up then—latecomers to the party of the century, literally—and Ashlee and Sydnee Southern got out, carrying more food.

Ashlee looked at Glitch shyly as she passed. Apparently they hadn't hooked up in this reality.

"Hi, Casey," she said, but Casey the Glitch was deep in thought and missed the whole thing. He tended to do things like that, and it would take the matchmaking talents of Brooke and me to get this ball rolling.

"I just have one question," he said, his brows drawn in meditation.

"Just one?" I still had a thousand. A million. A hundred million.

He nodded. "Yeah, just one for now." He narrowed his eyes on me and asked, "Why Glitch?"

BEAST

The next day, I found myself standing on a doorstep I never thought I would, which belonged to a friend I never thought I'd have. Tabitha opened the door. Her eyes widened in surprise; then she turned smug and derisive. Nice to see she was up to form and we hadn't been that great of friends after all. Clearly she was over me.

"Can I talk to you?" I asked.

She flipped her hair over a shoulder. "What about?"

"Please, Tabitha."

"Fine, whatever. Just get in here before someone sees you on my doorstep."

That was a quick turnaround. We went from being besties to mortal enemies in the blink of an eye. Worked for me. I'd honed my speech after the last three encounters. "Look, I'm a prophet. I can see things, okay? I can see into the future and the past, and I'm sorry, Tabitha, but when you brushed up against me once—" I bit down, hating to say what I had to say. "—I saw what happened to you last year. At that party."

"What are you talking about?" Then realization dawned on her pretty face. She stilled. "You need to leave."

"I will. But I just wanted you to know that no matter what you think, it wasn't your fault."

Her chin rose in defiance.

I stepped closer, close enough to make her uncomfortable. "It wasn't even a tiny bit your fault. None of it. And, for what it's worth, if you prosecute this guy, you will feel better in the long run, and you'll prevent him from doing the same thing to someone else."

Her eyes watered and she turned away from me, embarrassed. "That was a year ago. Even if I could convince a prosecutor of the truth, there's no evidence."

I knew it would come down to this. And now her self-esteem was about to take an even bigger beating. I toed the tile with the tip of my flats, not wanting to do this, but desperate times and all. "That's not entirely true. I promise you, that guy has irrefutable evidence of what happened."

"What? How can he possibly—?" When she figured it out, when the only answer to her questions slammed into her, she put a hand over her mouth. "Oh, my God, he recorded it." Her expression fixed on mortification.

"Tabitha, even if the recording doesn't prove beyond a

shadow of a doubt that you were forced against your will, you were fifteen. Fifteen, Tabitha. He was twenty-two. That right there is enough evidence to get him convicted of statutory rape, not to mention the fact that he plied you with alcohol. I'm pretty certain your parents will stop at nothing to see that man behind bars."

Again, her eyes widened, this time in horror. "I can't tell my parents." Her voice cracked and she covered her face. I could practically feel the heat of shame rushing through her. "I can't." Heart-wrenching sobs racked her body as the horror of her experience swallowed her again. She had trusted him. A boy from college whom she'd met at a football game. He'd been so sweet. So caring. He'd opened the door for her. Tucked her hair behind her ear. Convinced her to go to his dorm room.

I stepped forward and put a hand on her shoulder. She let me, and after a moment, she encircled me in her arms. She cried for several heartbreaking moments, her shoulders quaking with each sob, until I felt her mother would wait no longer. I stepped back, smiled reassuringly, and walked toward the door as she finally noticed the woman standing in the doorway to the kitchen, her mouth covered with the dish towel she'd been using, her expression full of compassion.

They would be okay. Tabitha would be okay, and I chose to see that as a positive thing.

I smiled when I spotted Jared across the street. Ever the diligent guardian. I guess, if this was the price I had to pay for saving the world, I'd just have to learn to live with it.

One week later, I woke up in the middle of the night and felt, for the first time, completely at ease in my surroundings. My room was gorgeous. I had to add some color, having no idea what I'd been thinking with everything so white. Maybe I'd been trying to sterilize my surroundings. To surround myself with cleanliness since being faced with a dirty alternative: the threat of war. The destruction of all things on earth. The deaths of everyone I knew and loved.

But we were living in a new time and I was beginning to embrace it. Jared had moved into the same apartment behind my grandparents' store after a major overhaul. Thankfully, just like last time, we had a plethora of men ready and willing to help out in the church. They worked tirelessly and had him moved in in three days. It was amazing what men would do to stay on the good side of the Angel of Death.

Because I couldn't get back to Maine, I'd actually had to tell Kenya over e-mail that she'd saved the world. Or, at the very least, helped save it. If she hadn't gone back for those photographs, I had no idea what would have happened.

She wrote me back. She didn't believe the memories until I contacted her. She was thrilled and excited and honored to have been a part of the war. But her recollection was fuzzy, and she asked me how she'd died. She remembered dying.

I lied in my next e-mail. How could I recount such a horrid event? I told her I didn't know. I told her I'd lost sight of her and when I'd looked back, she was gone. She wrote again, reminding me she carried a switchblade. I told her the truth in my third e-mail. As tough as she was, it was hard for her to hear.

We made plans for her to come to Riley's Switch in the summer. Her parents, the same parents who'd taught her all about me, about the prophecies and coming war, were beside themselves with glee at how everything had turned out. They wanted to meet me and my parents and my grandparents and the nephilim. They weren't certain about meeting the Angel of Death, but when I assured them he was on an Angel of Death hiatus, they agreed to meet him, too. Reluctantly.

After finding out exactly how much Kenya remembered, I told her to be wary of Wade, the stick figure–drawing maniac. She said it was already taken care of. He'd apparently started having visions of a different time, a different reality, and went stone crazy.

When asked if she had anything to do with his mental issues, Kenya pleaded the fifth.

I longed to see Crystal again. Kenya promised she was keeping an eye on her. In fact, they'd become very good friends. Crystal, unfortunately, didn't remember me. It seemed that only those with a direct connection to the events that day had the memories. So I asked Kenya if that were so, how did Wade remember?

She pleaded the fifth. Again.

I liked her.

For some odd reason, those were the things I thought about as I walked barefoot into the forest. The full moon helped light my path. My feet should have been cold. The forest floor should have cut as I walked across it. My gown should have been wet from the light droplets of rain I'd encountered earlier. And perhaps all of that was true, but I paid them no mind.

I strode deeper into the pine-scented woods, my feet padding along the damp ground, completely oblivious to anything but my goal. I stopped and listened for the breathing. I'd heard it for days. Or perhaps I'd simply felt it. Deep, heavy, and guttural, it echoed around me. What would have terrified any other trespasser only fueled my quest. I climbed up rocks, ducked under trees, and jumped over water until I came to a place in the forest that was dark. Unusually dark. Much darker than the surrounding area. It was like a black hole split the trees and opened a portal to another universe.

But I knew better. It was no hole. No portal. It was him. He'd come back for me. To be with me.

I stepped to him, placed my hand on his thick scales as he lay curled inside himself. He grunted, refusing to look at me like an impetuous child. I'd left him out here for days and he was angry, but slipping away from a nephilim and the Angel of Death was not as easy as one might think.

"How did you get out of hell?" I asked.

He stirred, then went back to his pouting, so I ran my hand along the bridge between his closed eyes. He smelled like lightning and soot, and his scales were as cold as an artic wind. His head, twice my height, possibly more, lay on a bed of pine needles. Add his horns, and his head alone was massive. I could only imagine how big the rest of him was. Then again, I didn't have to. I'd seen him. Twice. Once when I was six and once when I'd released him during the war. He was magnificent. A guardian of the underworld. Not evil, as we'd been led to believe, but guarding those who were evil, who were sent to what amounted to a prison in the afterlife.

"Well," I said to him, giving him one last chance to acknowledge me, "are you coming or not?"

He stirred and rose at last, his movements slow, labored as he unfolded to his full height. I looked up at him. His head topped the trees and blocked out the moon, which would not make navigating the forest any easier. He bent and ran a razor-sharp claw over my cheek, being careful not to scratch me. The damage that one claw could do was staggering, but it didn't concern me in the least. Not at the moment.

"I missed you, too," I said. Taking the claw into my hand, I said, "We better get back before my parents send out a search party."

He straightened again and followed me, taking one step to my thirty.

"I don't know how I'm going to explain you to Mom and Dad," I said as we traipsed back to my place. "Just try not to break anything."

A tree cracked and fell beside us, and branches sounded like popcorn, his broad shoulders snapping them like twigs as we passed, leaves and pine needles showering down around me.

I groaned aloud. This was not going to end well.

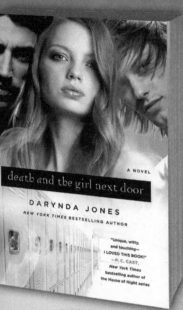